Dear Reader,

We're thrilled that some of Harlequin's most famous families are making an encore appearance! With this special Famous Families fifty-book collection, we are proud to offer you the chance to relive the drama, the glamour, the suspense and the romance of four of Harlequin's most beloved families—the Fortunes, the Bravos, the McCabes and the Cavanaughs.

Wedding bells are ringing for the infamous Bravos— even if they don't know it yet! The all-American clan created by *USA TODAY* bestselling author Christine Rimmer is the second family in our special collection. Its members are cowboys and billionaires, lawyers and private investigators. Their exploits take them from the mountains of Wyoming, to a small, close-knit town in California to the glitzy Vegas strip. But whether they're rich or down-to-earth, city or small-town bred, you'll fall in love with each of the Bravos as they take their own compelling journey to a happy ending.

And coming in May, you'll meet Dr. Jackson McCabe, as we introduce you to our next special family, the McCabes of Texas, by beloved author Cathy Gillen Thacker.

Happy reading,

The Editors

CHRISTINE RIMMER

came to her profession the long way around. Before settling down to write about the magic of romance, she'd been everything from an actress to a salesclerk to a waitress. Now that she's finally found work that suits her perfectly, she insists she never had a problem keeping a job—she was merely gaining "life experience" for her future as a novelist.

Christine is grateful not only for the joy she finds in writing, but for what waits when the day's work is through: a man she loves, who loves her right back, and the privilege of watching their children grow and change day to day. She lives with her family in Oregon. Visit Christine at www.christinerimmer.com.

FAMOUS FAMILIES

the BRAVOS

USA TODAY bestselling author

CHRISTINE RIMMER

The Millionaire She Married

TORONTO NEW YORK LONDON
AMSTERDAM PARIS SYDNEY HAMBURG
STOCKHOLM ATHENS TOKYO MILAN MADRID
PRAGUE WARSAW BUDAPEST AUCKLAND

For my dear friend Georgia Bockoven.
Thank you for the times you listened,
the useful advice
and the beautiful books you write.

Recycling programs
for this product may
not exist in your area.

ISBN-13: 978-0-373-36496-1

THE MILLIONAIRE SHE MARRIED

Copyright © 2000 by Christine Rimmer

Printed in U.S.A.

FAMOUS FAMILIES

The Fortunes

Cowboy at Midnight by Ann Major
A Baby Changes Everything by Marie Ferrarella
In the Arms of the Law by Peggy Moreland
Lone Star Rancher by Laurie Paige
The Good Doctor by Karen Rose Smith
The Debutante by Elizabeth Bevarly
Keeping Her Safe by Myrna Mackenzie
The Law of Attraction by Kristi Gold
Once a Rebel by Sheri WhiteFeather
Military Man by Marie Ferrarella
Fortune's Legacy by Maureen Child
The Reckoning by Christie Ridgway

The Bravos by Christine Rimmer

The Nine-Month Marriage
Marriage by Necessity
Practically Married
Married by Accident
The Millionaire She Married
The M.D. She Had to Marry
The Marriage Agreement
The Bravo Billionaire
The Marriage Conspiracy
His Executive Sweetheart
Mercury Rising
Scrooge and the Single Girl

Chapter 1

The shop, like the steep, rather narrow street it stood on, had a feel of times past about it. The oyster-white sign over the door read Linen and Lace in flowing script. Vines and morning glories twined and trailed in and out of the lettering.

Mack McGarrity stood beneath a striped awning, his hands fisted in his pockets, staring in the window to the left of the shop's entrance. Beyond the glass was a brass canopy bed. The bed was draped with lacy white curtains, covered in filmy white linens and piled with embroidered white pillows.

Next to the bed, on the left, stood a white dresser bearing a white pitcher and bowl. On the right, a white nightstand, with a vase of white roses and a white-shaded lamp. White lacy nightgowns, each one a little different from the next, had been tossed in an artful tangle across the pillows and the filmy bedcovers, as if the lady who owned them all couldn't make up her mind which to wear.

Mack smiled to himself. The fists stuck in his pockets relaxed a little.

On their wedding night Jenna had worn a nightgown like one of those thrown across that white bed—an almost transparent gown, with lace at the collar and down the front. And roses, little pink ones, embroidered around the tiny pearly buttons.

Those buttons had given him trouble. They were so damn small. And he *had* been nervous, though he'd tried not to show it.

But Jenna had known.

And she'd laughed, that soft, teasing laugh of hers. "It's not as if it's our first time," she'd whispered.

"It *is* the first time. *My* first time…with my wife." His voice had been gruff, he remembered, gruff with emotions he'd never allowed anyone but Jenna to see….

Mack turned from the window. He stared across the street, at a store that sold hand-painted furniture. A man and a woman stood at the display window there, admiring a tall bureau decorated with a woodland scene. Mack watched them, not really seeing them, until they disappeared inside.

Then, rather abruptly, he turned back to the shop called Linen and Lace. Two determined steps later, he reached the glass-fronted door. He took the handle and pulled it open.

The scent of the place hit him first—floral, sweet but not too sweet. An undertone of tartness. And something spicy, too. Like cinnamon. It didn't smell like Jenna, exactly. But it reminded him of her. Sweet and just a little spicy.

He'd barely started to smile at the thought when he realized he'd tripped the buzzer that would warn her she had another customer. She turned and saw him just as he spotted her.

When the buzzer rang, Jenna glanced toward the door out of habit, ready to send her new customer a swift, be-right-with-you smile.

The smile died unborn on her lips.

It was Mack.

Mack.

Her ex-husband. Here. In her shop.

After all these years.

It couldn't be.

But it was. Definitely.

Mack.

Her throat closed up on itself. She gulped to keep from gasping.

He looked…terrific. Older, yes. And somehow more relaxed. But in a deep and fundamental way, the same.

He was staring straight at her through those eyes she remembered much too well. Not quite blue and not quite gray, like a sky caught between sunshine and cloudiness.

He smiled at her—that beautiful, half ironic, half shy smile, the one that had dropped her in her tracks nine years before.

He'd lived in an apartment down the hall from her. And she had knocked on his door to tell him that she knew very well he'd been feeding her cat.

When he answered, he actually held Byron in his arms. That sleek midnight-black traitor had the nerve to purr as if he belonged there.

"I'll have you know, that's my cat," she'd informed him, doing her best to sound bold.

He had smiled, just the way he was smiling at her now—like the sun coming out on a gray, chilly day. She'd felt the warmth, a warmth that reached down inside her and then started to spread.

"Come on in," he had suggested as he stroked her cat. "We'll talk about it."

It had never even occurred to her to say no.

And now, all these years later, just the sight of him made her feel as if something inside her was melting. Her knees wanted to wobble; her pulse knocked in her ears.

Along with the weakness, the unconscionable excitement, she also knew dread.

Why had he come here?

When she had called him three days before, she'd asked one thing of him—made one simple, very clear request. He had said that he would take care of it.

Did his sudden appearance in her shop mean that he had changed his mind?

"Er...miss? Are you all right?"

Jenna snapped her head around and forced a brilliant smile for her customer. "I am fine. Where were we?" She glanced down at the stack of brightly colored linens she clutched in her arms. "Ah, of course. I remember. And I do understand. Not everyone loves white. That's why I wanted you to see these. They're by an English designer I especially like. Summer Garden is the name of this pattern. Beautiful, isn't it? The colors are so vivid, different intensities of green and blue, with the flowers like splashes of pink and yellow and red." She held out the neatly folded pile of sheets. "Feel."

Her customer ran a hand over the fabric. "Soft."

"And durable, too. Three hundred thread count. The finest quality combed cotton, cool in summer, cozy in winter." Jenna slid a glance at Mack. He was watching her. Waiting.

And he'll just have to wait a little longer, she thought. "Come this way." She indicated a display near the far wall. "I have more from this designer. Tell me what you think...."

A few minutes later, Jenna closed a sale of sheets, pillowcases, shams and a comforter. As soon as she rang that one up, there was someone new to wait on. And someone else after that. Since one of her clerks had the day off and the other had taken a two-hour lunch in order to handle a few personal errands, all the customers were Jenna's. And Jenna never liked to make a customer wait.

Still, she could have stolen a moment for the civilities, a moment for hello-how-are-you. An opportunity to find out why Mack had come. She didn't do that. Because she was stalling, foolishly hoping he might just give up and leave.

But no. He wandered the room, examining her merchandise as if he actually intended to buy something. He seemed...very patient, quite willing to wait until she had time to deal with him.

His patience bothered her almost as much as his sudden appearance in her shop. The Mack she had known had been far from a patient man.

But things *had* changed since then. Back then, Mack McGarrity had been a man on a mission. He'd been determined to carve out his niche in the world and he'd driven himself relentlessly toward that goal. Now he had millions.

Maybe having lots of money meant you could afford even more than a mansion in the Florida Keys and a forty-six-foot fishing boat. Maybe having lots of money meant you could afford to wait.

Or at least, maybe it had done that for Mack McGarrity.

The thought probably should have pleased her. For a man like Mack to learn patience—that was a good thing.

But it didn't please her. It made her nervous. Mack had always been relentless. To think that he might now be patient as well could cause her considerable difficulty if, for some reason, he decided to use those characteristics against her.

But why would he do that?

She didn't want to know—which was why she kept stalling, kept letting him wait.

Nearly an hour after Mack entered the shop, Jenna found herself alone with him—save for an elderly woman who came in often to browse. The nice old lady took her time, as usual. Finally she settled on a three-piece set of needlepoint antimacassars. Jenna rang up the sale and counted out change.

"Thank you so much. Come back again," Jenna said as she walked her customer to the door.

"Oh, you know I will, dear. I love your little shop." A cagey grin appeared on the woman's puckered rosebud of a mouth. "And you always do pay such lovely attention to me when I visit."

Jenna pulled open the door. To the accompaniment of the shop's buzzer, her customer toddled outside, turning to wave as she made her way up the street. Jenna stepped onto the sidewalk to wave back. Stalling.

And then the time had come. Jenna went inside again and shut the door.

Mack had moved into the central aisle, only a few feet away from her. She felt cornered, so near the door that she kept triggering the buzzer, but distressingly reluctant to move closer to him.

He had the courtesy to back up a few paces. She moved warily toward him and the buzzing ceased.

There was silence.

She had to force herself to say his name. "Hello, Mack."

"Hello, Jenna."

She stared into his face, a tanned face now, with the creases around the eyes a little deeper than before. His light brown hair was still cut no-nonsense short, but more time in the sun had given it gold highlights. His eyebrows, too, had gone gold at the tips.

He looked good. He really did.

And she had been staring too long. She cut her eyes away, not sure what to say next.

She wanted to demand, "What are you doing here? To order, Go away, and don't come back." To insist, "I have my own life now. I *run* my own life. It's a good life, and it doesn't include you."

But she knew that if she said those things, she would only sound defensive, would only put herself at a disadvantage right from the start. So the uncomfortable silence continued for several more agonizing seconds.

At last he spoke. "Struck speechless at the sight of me, huh?"

She met his eyes directly, sucked in a breath and

forced out a brisk reply. "Well, I have to admit, I don't understand why you're here. Key West is a long way from Meadow Valley, California."

Key West. She never would have believed it. Mack, the ultimate workaholic lawyer, living in the tropics, drifting around the Gulf of Mexico in that boat of his. The idea of her driven, success-obsessed husband—correction, *ex*-husband—drifting *anywhere* seemed a complete contradiction in terms.

And she wished he'd quit looking at her with that amused and embarrassingly knowing expression, quit making her feel so…young and awkward. As if she were twenty-one again, a lonely college girl far from home, instead of the mature, settled, self-possessed thirty she was now.

What was it about him? How did he do it? It had been seven years since she'd seen him face-to-face, and five since their divorce should have been final. Still, right now, staring at him, with him staring back at her, she felt exposed. Raw. As if the mere sight of him had ripped open old and still-festering wounds—wounds she'd been certain had healed long ago.

It had been hard enough to pick up the phone and call him, after tracking him down through one of his colleagues at his old law firm. Hard enough to talk to him again, to hear his voice, to ask him to send her the papers she needed.

When she'd hung up, she'd told herself, Well, at least *that's* done.

But now here she was. Face-to-face with him, feeling raw and wounded. Breathless and confused.

It shouldn't be like this, and she knew it. All the hurt

and recriminations were long past, not to mention the yearning, the tenderness, the *love.*

By now she should be able to smile at him, to feel reasonably at ease, to ask calmly if he'd brought her the papers.

The papers. Yes. That was the question.

She cleared her throat. "Did you...decide to bring the papers in person, is that it? It really wasn't necessary, Mack. Not necessary at all."

He didn't reply immediately, only kept looking at her. Looking at her so intently, causing that weakness in her knees and a certain disturbing fluttering in her solar plexus.

Now she wanted to shout at him, "Answer me! Where are those papers?"

But then the buzzer sounded again. Jenna glanced over her shoulder, pasted on a smile. "I'll be right with you."

"No hurry." The new customer, a well-dressed, forty-ish woman, detoured toward a display of afghans and furniture scarves hung from quilt stands along the side wall.

Jenna looked back at Mack. He glanced toward the woman over by the afghans, then spoke in a low voice. "I want to talk to you. Alone."

"No!" The word came out all wrong. It sounded frantic and desperate.

"Yes." Lower still and very soft. Gentle. Yet utterly unyielding.

"Miss?" The customer was fingering the fringe of a piano shawl. "There's no price tag on this one."

Jenna realized she was scowling. As she glanced toward her customer, she rearranged her face into a bright smile. "I'll be right there. Just one moment." She turned to Mack again, the cheerful smile mutating instantly back to a scowl. "We have nothing to say to each other."

"I think we do."

"You can't just—" Her voice had risen. She cut herself off, got herself back under control, then went on in an intense whisper. "You can't just wander in here after all these years and expect me to—"

"Jenna." He reached out and snared her right hand.

Before she could think to jerk away, he tugged her behind a wrought-iron shelving unit stacked with Egyptian-cotton towels and accessories for the bath. Vaguely stunned that he had actually touched her, she looked down at their joined hands.

"Let go," she instructed in a furious whisper.

He did, which stunned her all over again, somehow. One moment his big warm hand surrounded hers—and the next, it was gone.

He said, "I'm not expecting anything. I only want to talk to you. In private."

She could see it in his eyes, in the set of his jaw. He was not going to just go away. She would have to deal with him, to listen to whatever he'd decided he had to say to her.

Right then, guiltily, she thought of Logan, her high school sweetheart, her dear friend—and now, her fiancé. Logan had waited a long time to make her his bride. And when this little problem with her divorce from Mack had cropped up, Logan, as usual, had been the soul of understanding. He hadn't reproached her, hadn't asked her how she'd managed, over five whole years, to let it slip her mind that she'd never received her copy of the final divorce decree.

He'd just gently suggested that she get the situation cleared up.

So she'd called Mack.

And Mack had said that he did have the papers and he would sign them, have them notarized and send them to her right away. So she'd reported to Logan that everything had been worked out. When the papers came, in the next few days, she would file them. Within six months she and Logan would be free to marry.

Logan hadn't been thrilled about the waiting period required by California law. But he had accepted it gracefully.

She wasn't so certain how he'd accept the news that Mack had appeared in person and demanded to speak with her *in private.*

But then again, maybe he wouldn't even have to know about this little problem until after it had been resolved.

Logan, who was an M.D. in family practice, had left two days ago for a medical convention in Seattle. He wouldn't return until Sunday night—two more days from now.

By then, Jenna told herself, she'd have everything under control. By then, she would have listened to whatever Mack had to say, taken the papers from him and sent him on his way. The whole situation would be much easier to explain to her fiancé once she had the papers in her hands.

"Miss?" It was the woman over by the afghans, beginning to sound a bit put out.

"Go ahead," Mack said. "Take care of her."

The woman bought the piano scarf. Mack waited, standing a little to the side of the register counter, as Jenna rang up the sale.

Once her customer had left, Jenna sighed and conceded, "All right. I close up at seven. After that, we can talk."

"Good," Mack said. "There are a couple of promising-looking restaurants down the street. I'll drop back by when you close and we'll get something to eat."

Not on your life, she thought. She would not spend the evening sitting across a table from him, fighting the feeling that they were out on a date.

"No," she said. "Come to the house at seven-thirty. We can talk there. Lacey's visiting for a while, but she won't bother us."

"Lacey." He said her younger sister's name with more interest than he'd ever shown in the past. "Visiting? From where?"

"She lives in Los Angeles now."

"What does she do there, rob banks?"

Jenna gave him a too-sweet smile. "She's an artist. And a very talented one, too."

"Still the rebel, you mean."

"Lacey makes her own rules."

"I believe it—and how's your mom?"

Jenna didn't answer immediately. Sometimes she still found it hard to believe that Margaret Bravo was gone. "She died two years ago."

He looked at her for a long moment before muttering, "I'm sorry, Jenna."

He'd hardly given a thought to Jenna's mother while she was alive. Mack McGarrity didn't put much store in family ties. But right now he did sound sincere. Jenna murmured a reluctant "Thank you," then spoke more briskly. "Seven-thirty, then. My house."

"I'll be there."

"Bring the divorce papers. You *do* have those papers?"

"I've got them."

He had the papers. Relief washed through her. Maybe this wouldn't be as bad as she'd feared.

Chapter 2

Jenna walked home from the shop. It was only three blocks to the big Queen Anne Victorian at the top of West Broad Street where she'd grown up. She enjoyed the walk. She waved to her neighbors and breathed the faint scent of pine in the air and thought about how much she loved her hometown. Tucked into a pocket of the Sierra foothills, Meadow Valley was a charming place of steep, tree-lined streets and tidy, old, wood-frame houses.

At home, Jenna found the note Lacey had left on the refrigerator.

"Last-minute hot date. Don't wait up."

Jenna grinned to herself at the words scrawled in her sister's bold hand. When Lacey said, "Don't wait up," she meant it. Since about the age of eleven, Jenna's "baby" sister had never willingly gone to bed before 2:00 a.m. Lacey loved staying up so late that she could watch the sun rise before calling it a night.

Jenna's grin became a frown.

Without Lacey, she and Mack would be alone in the house.

She crumpled the note and turned for the trash bin beneath the sink. She saw Byron then. He was sitting on the floor to the right of the sink cabinet door, his long, black tail wrapped neatly around his front paws.

"I don't want to be alone with him," Jenna said to the cat. "And do not ask me why."

The cat didn't, only regarded her through those wise yellow-green eyes of his. "Don't look at me like that," she scolded as she tossed the note into the trash bin and shoved the cabinet door shut.

The cat went on looking, beginning to purr now, the sound quite loud in the quiet kitchen. Byron never had talked much. But he could purr with the best of them.

Jenna scooped him up and put him on her shoulder. "If you fall all over yourself rubbing on him, I'll never forgive you." She stroked the sleek raven fur, and the cat purred all the louder. "I mean it," she grumbled, but the cat remained unconcerned.

"All right, all right. Dinner for you." She scooped food into his bowl, then left him to his meal.

In the downstairs master bedroom she changed from her linen jacket and bias-cut rayon skirt into Dockers and a camp shirt. She purposely did not freshen up her makeup one bit or even run a comb through her straight, shoulder-length blond hair.

And when she returned to the kitchen for a tall glass of iced tea, she pointedly did not rush around whipping up a little something to tempt a man's palate. She was not dressing up for Mack and he was getting no dinner. She had one order of business to transact with him.

She wanted the final divorce papers he was supposed to have signed five and a half years ago. And then she wanted him back in Florida where he belonged.

Ten minutes later she answered the doorbell. It was Mack, grinning that knee-weakening grin of his. A pair of waiters stood behind him.

She blinked. *Waiters?* Yes. Definitely. Waiters. In crisp white shirts, black slacks and neat black bow ties. One carried a round table with a pedestal base, the other had a chair under each arm.

"What in the—?"

"You didn't cook, did you? Well, if you did, save it. I've brought dinner with me."

"But I— You— I don't—"

"You're stammering," he said with nerve-flaying fondness. Then he gestured at the waiters. "This way— Jenna, sweetheart, you'll have to move aside."

"I am not your—"

"Sorry. Old habits. Now, get out of the way."

He stepped forward, took her by the shoulders and guided her back from the door. Then he gestured at the waiters again. They followed him into the front parlor, where they proceeded to set up the table on her mother's hand-hooked Roosevelt Star rug.

In the ensuing seven or eight minutes, Jenna tried to tell Mack a number of times that she wasn't having dinner with him. He pretended not to hear her as the waiters trekked back and forth from a van out in the front, bringing linens and dishes and flatware and a centerpiece of flower-shaped candles floating in a cut-crystal bowl. They also brought in a side table and set it up under the front window. They put the food there. It looked and smelled sinfully delicious.

When all was in readiness, one waiter lit the candles as the other pulled out Jenna's chair for her.

Jenna sent a glare at Mack. "I don't like this."

He put on an innocent expression, which she did not buy for a nanosecond. "Come on, Jenna. It's only dinner."

The waiter waited, holding the chair.

Jenna gave in and sat down, thinking that Mack McGarrity might have managed to develop a little patience, he even might have learned how to relax. But in this, he hadn't changed at all. He still insisted on doing things one hundred percent his way.

Mack slid into the chair opposite her. He gestured to the waiters and one of them set a bread basket on the table, along with two plates of tempting appetizers: stuffed miniature portobello mushrooms and oysters on the half shell, nestled in chipped ice. The other waiter busied himself opening a bottle of pinot grigio, which Mack sampled, approved and then poured for Jenna and for himself.

That done, Mack signed the check.

The moment the front door closed behind the waiters, Jenna placed one mushroom and one oyster on her plate. She also buttered a warm slice of sourdough bread. Then she rose from her chair. She dished up more food from the offerings on the side table—a good-sized helping of *salade niçoise* and a modest serving of sautéed veal scallops with marsala sauce.

She sat down and ate. The appetizers were as good as they looked, as were the salad and the veal. She did not touch her wine.

As she methodically chewed and swallowed, Mack kept trying to get her talking. He asked about her shop and complimented her on the changes she'd made in the decor of her mother's front parlor. He wondered aloud where Lacey was and tried to get her to tell him more about her sister's life as a struggling artist in Southern California.

Jenna answered in single syllables whenever possible. When the question absolutely required a longer answer, she gave him a whole sentence—and then went back to her meal.

She was finished ten minutes after she'd started. She pushed her plate away. "Thank you, Mack. That was excellent."

"I'm so glad you enjoyed it," he muttered, finishing off his glass of wine and reaching for the bottle again.

She granted him a sour smile. "You've hardly eaten." He'd taken one mushroom and a single breadstick.

"For some reason, I feel rushed. It's ruined my appetite." He poured more wine, set the bottle down.

Jenna smoothed her napkin in at the side of her plate. "Well, then. If you don't feel like eating, then maybe we can proceed to the main order of business here."

He was staring at her engagement diamond. "Nice ring," he muttered.

"Thank you. I like it, too—and can we talk about what you supposedly came here to talk about?"

He gestured with his wineglass. "By all means."

She straightened her shoulders and inched her chin up a notch. "As I told you on the phone, I want to get married again."

"Congratulations." Mack took a minute to sip from his glass. Then he lowered the glass and looked at her straight on. "But don't you think you ought to get rid of your first husband before you start talking about taking on another one?"

"I *am* rid of my first husband," she replied in a carefully controlled tone. "Or I was supposed to be. Everything was settled."

"For you, maybe."

She glared at him. "It *was* settled, Mack."

He grunted. "Whatever you say."

"Well, all right. I *say* that everything was over—except that, for some reason, you never got around to signing the papers that my lawyer sent your lawyer."

Mack studied the depths of his wineglass for a moment, then looked at her once more. "It was a busy time for me. I had a lot on my mind."

She decided to let his lame excuses pass. "The point is, it's over, Mack. Long over. And you know it. I don't know why you're here, after all these years. I don't *care* why you're here."

He sat up a little straighter. "I don't believe that."

"Believe what you want. Just—" *Give me those papers and get out of my life!* she wanted to shout. But she didn't. She paused. She gathered her composure, then asked quite civilly, "Do you have the papers?"

He brought his wineglass to his lips again and regarded her broodingly over the rim. "Not with me."

Jenna could quite easily have picked up the crystal bowl of floating candles from the center of the table and heaved it at his head. To keep herself from doing that, she folded her hands in her lap and spoke with measured care. "You said you had the papers."

"And I do. I just didn't bring them with me tonight."

"You lied."

"I didn't lie. *You* heard what you wanted to hear."

Another lie, she thought, but held her tongue this time. She'd lived with Mack McGarrity long enough to recognize a verbal trap when he laid one. If she kept insisting that he'd lied, they'd only end up going around and around, her accusing and him denying, getting nowhere.

Let it go, she thought. *Move on.* She said, "You told me you wanted to talk to me. In private. Well, here we are. Just the way you wanted it. You'd better start talking, Mack. You'd better tell me what is going on."

He set his glass on the table. "Jenna, I—" He cut himself off. Something across the room had caught his eye. She followed his glance to the black cat peeking around the edge of the arch that led to the formal dining room. "My God. Is that…?"

"Byron," she provided reluctantly, at the same time as he whispered, "Bub?"

The cat's lean body slid around the arch. Then, his long tail high, Byron strutted over, jumped lightly onto Mack's lap, lay down and began to purr in obvious contentment. Mack petted the black fur in long, slow strokes. Jenna looked away, furious with him for this game he was playing—and moved in spite of her fury at the sight of him with Byron again after all these years.

She stared out the front window at the Boston fern hanging from the eaves of the porch as the sound of Byron's happy purring rumbled in her ears. When she looked back, Mack was watching her. His eyes were soft now, full of memories, of dangerous tenderness. "He has some gray around his neck."

Jenna's throat felt uncomfortably tight. "He's not a young cat. He was full-grown when we found him."

She thought of their first meeting again, though she

shouldn't have allowed herself such a foolish indulgence.

Nine years ago. It seemed like forever.

And also, like yesterday...

She'd been in her junior year, majoring in business administration at UCLA. And he'd been twenty-five, just finishing law school.

Once he'd led her into his apartment, he'd informed her that the cat had adopted him.

"No," she had argued, "That cat adopted *me,* the first day I moved in, three weeks ago."

They were in his living room, which had a shortage of furniture and an excess of books—they were everywhere, overflowing the board-and-block bookcases, in piles on the floor. He petted Byron and he looked at her, a look that made her feel warm and weak and absolutely wonderful. He introduced himself. And he said that he'd named the cat Bub.

She had demanded, "You named my cat Bub?"

"It's *my* cat."

"No, he's mine. And Bub. What kind of a name is that?"

"A better name than Byron—which is just the kind of name a woman would give a black cat."

"Byron fits my cat perfectly."

"No. This cat is no Byron. This cat is a Bub."

"No, his name is Byron. And he's mine."

"No, he's mine."

"I beg your pardon. He is mine."

And about then, Mack suggested, "We could share...." He said the words quietly, looking deep in her eyes, stroking Byron's silky fur and smiling a smile that made her want to find something sturdy to lean against.

"Share...?"

He nodded.

Further discussion had followed. She could no longer remember all that had been said. The words hadn't really mattered anyway. There was his voice asking and her voice answering, his eyes looking into hers, the feeling that she'd knocked on a door—his door—and found a different world waiting beyond the threshold. A magical, shimmering, golden world. A world with Mack McGarrity in it.

In the end, it was agreed. They would share Byron— Bub, as Mack called him. Mack suggested they have dinner together to celebrate. It sounded like a lovely idea to Jenna.

They ate at an inexpensive Italian restaurant not far from their apartment building. And when they returned to his place, he'd asked her in for a last cup of coffee.

She'd stayed, after the coffee. She'd spent the night in his bed—well, actually, on his mattress on the floor. At that time, Mack McGarrity couldn't afford things like beds.

It had been her first time. And it had been beautiful. And after that night, she had moved in with him. Two months later, on November 10, they were married. Jenna had thought herself the luckiest, happiest woman on earth....

"Jenna." Mack was looking at her now, over the shimmering flames of those candles afloat in that cut-crystal bowl. The cat went on purring, and the past seemed a living thing, as real as the cat and the glowing candle flames, a presence in her mother's front parlor with them.

He said, "Since you called, I've been thinking…."

No, she thought. *Don't say it. Please don't.*

But he did. "You can't marry the med student, Jenna. Not yet."

The med student.

Logan.

Oh, God. What was the matter with her? Taking this dangerous little mental detour down memory lane? Letting herself forget Logan, who loved her and treated her with respect and understanding. Who wanted exactly the same things that she wanted: a partner for life, an *equal* partner. And a big family. Lots of children. Three or four at the very least.

"Logan is not a med student anymore," she informed the infuriating man across the table from her. "Years have passed, Mack, just in case you didn't notice."

He had stopped petting Byron. Those blue-gray eyes bored into hers. "I have noticed, as a matter of fact."

"Logan's finished med school." Her throat felt so tight, it hurt. She swallowed, made herself go on. "He's…done his internship and his residency. He's a full-fledged M.D. in family practice right here in Meadow Valley."

"I don't care if he's Jonas Salk. You can't marry him right now."

She couldn't sit still for that. And she didn't. She shot to her feet. "This is just like you," she accused through clenched teeth. "You appear out of nowhere after all these years and you immediately start telling me how I'm going to run my life. Well, I'm not going to do what you tell me to do anymore. I want those papers you promised you'd sign, Mack. And I want them now."

"I didn't promise."

"That is a lie. You told me on the phone that you would—"

"I know what I said."

"Good. Because what you said was that you'd sign the papers and send them right to me."

"You caught me off guard."

"It doesn't matter how I caught you. You said—"

He waved a hand, then used it to resume stroking her cat. "You'll get what you want. But not right this minute."

I will not start yelling, she silently vowed. *No matter how tempting the prospect may be, I will not begin screaming at him.*

She asked, "What does that mean—not right this minute?"

"It means I want a little time with you first."

"Time?" It came out as a croak.

"Yes. Time."

Oh, sweet Lord, she did not like the sound of this. She did not like it in the least. She strove mightily for calm—and did somehow manage to keep her voice even. "Time for what?"

Byron chose that moment to leave Mack's lap. The tag on his collar jingled as he jumped to the floor. Landing neatly on the balls of his dainty feet, he strutted across the room, then sat down beneath a marble-topped mahogany side table, where he began bathing himself. Mack watched him.

"Mack," Jenna demanded, to get his attention. He looked at her again. She repeated, "Time for what?"

He studied her before he spoke, his expression arranged into what she always used to think of as his lawyer's face. Composed. Aloof. All-knowing. His eyes looked out from beneath the golden shelf of his brow, seeing everything, revealing nothing.

He said, "We had something good once. And I admit it was mostly my fault that we lost it. I want some time to try to understand what went wrong."

Conflicting emotions swirled inside her. Confusion. Rage. A strange and rather frightening giddiness.

She longed to sit down again, to let her knees crumple and drop to her chair. But she remained upright. "Mack. I just want the signed papers. Please."

And he just sat there, looking out at her through those totally unrevealing lawyer's eyes. "As I said, you'll have them. After you spend two weeks with me."

She gulped. *"Two weeks?"*

"That's right. Two weeks. Alone with me."

She did sit down then. And once seated, she closed her eyes and raked her hair back from her face. "Mack. You cannot do this. I'll…divorce you all over again."

His lips curved, just slightly, as if he found that remark amusing, but only vaguely so. "You're not serious."

She forced total conviction into her reply. "I certainly am."

He reached out and picked up his wineglass again. "Divorcing me all over again will take time." He sipped, settling back in his chair. "It took over a year before, from the date that your lawyer first contacted mine until we reached a settlement. And then we were only fighting over Bub."

Ridiculous, she thought, remembering. Ridiculous

and petty. She'd been back home in Meadow Valley when she'd filed, and he was still in New York with that high-powered law firm. He'd hired one of the lawyers from his own firm and instructed him to demand "custody" of Byron. For months, his lawyer and hers had corresponded. And then, out of nowhere, Mack had decided to be reasonable. He'd let her have Byron. Everything had been settled.

All he'd had to do was sign the blasted papers, and everything would have been fine.

He sipped some more. "This time I could fix it so it takes forever. I hope the good doctor will wait for you. But then, I suppose he will. I remember him, how he hung around that one Christmas we spent here. He was waiting for you even way back then—when there was no doubt at all you were another man's wife."

Desperate, Jenna tried another threat—anything, she thought, to make him back down. "I'll get a big chunk of your money if I divorce you now."

He grunted in disbelief and sipped more wine. "Oh, come on. I know you, Jenna. Except for Bub, you wouldn't take anything six years ago. And you won't take anything now."

She gave him her best level-eyed stare. "Don't bet on it. I'm a lot meaner than I used to be. And besides, you weren't a multimillionaire when I divorced you. You were just a lawyer in a big firm, killing yourself and ignoring your wife, spending every waking minute clawing your way to the top. Now you're so rich, I might not be able to resist making a bid for half of all you've got."

"So." He was smiling again. "You know how much money I've got."

The truth was, she *had* followed the stories about him. "I have a pretty good idea."

"From whom?"

She shrugged. "I read the newspapers."

Six years ago, Mack had taken on a class-action suit against a major automobile manufacturer, a suit no one else in his firm had been willing to touch. He'd ended up going out on his own to handle it. And his share of the final settlement had come to ten million dollars.

He advised with some irony, "If you're after my money, you'll be happy to hear that I've at least doubled the ten million I started out with."

"I'm sure you're a very wise investor."

"No, I take big chances. And they pay off."

"Well. Good." She stabbed the air with her index finger. "That means more for me when I take you to the cleaners—which I will, Mack. I swear I will."

He regarded her for an endless count of five. She glared right back at him, thinking how easy it would be to pick up her dinner knife and hurl it at his heart.

At last he said in a musing tone, "You've developed a temper. I don't remember you having a temper before. You were sweet and shy. And you cried instead of getting mad."

She pushed back her chair again and stood. It felt a lot better, looking down on him. "Right. I used to be a wimp. But now I'm all grown up. I make my own decisions. And I have a life. Do you understand that? There is a man I want to marry and a business I need to run. I can't leave my store for two weeks. And I certainly can't leave my fiancé to run off with another man."

"Not just any other man, Jenna. Your husband."

"You are not my husband, not in any but a purely technical sense."

He lifted a brow at her, insolently, as if her assertion didn't even deserve comment. "I'm sure you can find someone to look after your store."

"I am not going to find anyone, because I'm not going anywhere."

He set his half-finished glass of wine on the table and rose slowly to his feet. "Just leave all this right where it is. The restaurant will send someone over tomorrow morning to deal with it." He pulled a business card from his back pocket and set it on the table. "Call this number. Tell them what time you want them to show up."

She didn't even glance at that card. She looked right at the maddening man standing across the table from her. "I am not—repeat, *not*—spending two weeks with you, Mack."

The look he gave her then was almost tender. "Think about it, Jenna. Two weeks isn't that long. We'll go to my place in Key West. I think you'll like it there. The house is old, like this one. It needs…a woman's touch."

"Hire a decorator."

He didn't reply to that, only looked at her indulgently before adding, "Once the two weeks are over, you'll be rid of me for good—unless we both decide we shouldn't be divorced after all."

She couldn't hold back one sharp, disdainful cry. "I don't need two weeks to decide that. I decided that a long time ago."

He actually had the gall to pretend to be wounded. "You're really hurting my feelings here."

She gaped at him, wondering how he could joke

about this. It was not funny. Not funny in the least. "This is…blackmail. It's…it's kidnapping. It has to be illegal."

He shook his head. "It's not. Trust me. I know. I'm a lawyer."

"Mack. Please." She pulled out all the stops and stooped to pleading. "*Please.* There is no point in this. Don't you see? Nothing good can come of it. I don't want to…to reconcile with you. It's over for me. And even if it wasn't, how can you possibly imagine that forcing me to go away with you would somehow make me change my mind?"

"Answer me this. Is there *anything* that would make you change your mind?"

"Absolutely not."

"Then this is the only option I've got."

"That's insane. I just told you it can't work."

"Maybe you're wrong. And since you have no other suggestions…"

"Suggestions? You want suggestions? What about keeping your word? What about giving me those papers and going back where you belong?"

He shook his head. "Uh-uh."

"Mack. I don't want to get back together with you. And I do *not* want to spend two weeks alone with you."

"But you will spend two weeks with me. If you want those divorce papers."

"Mack, be reasonable. You have to see that doing this will get you nowhere."

He smiled, a rueful smile. "I'm staying at the Northern Empire Inn. Give me a call when you're ready to agree to my terms."

Chapter 3

The phone rang at nine. It was Logan, calling from his hotel room in Seattle. He said that he was learning more about the advances in the treatment of childhood infections than his practice could afford. There was a certain very pricey piece of state-of-the-art equipment he wanted to buy.

As he talked, Jenna tried to keep her mind on what he was saying, tried not to think about Mack, about how angry she was, how trapped she felt. About what in the world she was going to do now.

"Jenna? You still with me?"

"Of course. I'm right here. How's the food there—and are you getting enough sleep?"

"The food? I've had worse. And yes, I'm getting plenty of sleep. What about you? Miss me?"

"Desperately."

He chuckled. "Don't overplay it. I'll become suspicious."

Suspicious. Oh, Lord. If he only knew.

And he *should* know. She would have to tell him.

But not now. Not on the phone from seven hundred miles away.

She'd tell him when she could sit down with him, face-to-face, after he returned home.

He asked, "So what are you and Lacey up to tonight?"

"We're not. I came home and there was a note on the fridge. A hot date, it said."

"I didn't know Lacey was seeing someone in Meadow Valley."

"I don't think she is. It's probably just one of her old high school friends, Mira or Maud—or maybe both."

"The terrible twins. Scary." He spoke jokingly. But he wasn't joking, not really. Logan had never approved of Lacey's old friends. He didn't much approve of Lacey, either, though he always treated her kindly, partly for Jenna's sake and also because he liked to think of himself as Lacey's "honorary" older brother.

"The twins are all grown up now," Jenna reminded him. "And they've settled down considerably. They haven't spray-painted obscenities on high school walls or gotten caught breaking and entering for years. Maud's married and a mother—and a darn good one, from what I hear."

"That's reassuring," Logan muttered drily. "Seriously. Is Lacey all right? She seemed a little…subdued the other day." Logan had been at the house when Lacey had first arrived from L.A.

"She's fine. Just taking a break from the rat race, she said. A few weeks in her hometown. Some rest and relaxation. Oh, and she also mentioned that a certain gallery owner had been talking about showcasing her work. Evidently the deal fell through somehow."

"A disappointment." His tone was knowing.

"That's what it sounded like to me. So if she seems a little down, that's probably why."

"She'll get over it."

"Of course she will."

"What she ought to do is get a *real* job. She's twenty-five years old, after all. Time to make a few realistic decisions. There's no reason she couldn't move back to Meadow Valley permanently. That house of your mother's is half hers now. As soon as you and I get married, she could have it to herself. Plenty of room to set up a studio and paint in her spare time. She ought to—"

"Logan," Jenna cut in gently.

He was silent, then he chuckled. "I know, I know. None of my business. But she *is* your sister. And I worry about her."

"I know you do. And it's very sweet of you."

"Tell me again how much you miss me." She could picture the loving smile on his handsome face. The image made her feel about two inches tall.

"Jenna? Are you there?"

"I miss you," she said. "A lot. And I..." Her throat closed up. She had to swallow before she could get the words out. "I love you. Very much."

"And I love you, Jenna Bravo. Did you get those papers in the mail from Florida yet?"

"Uh. No. No, I'm afraid that I didn't."

"Well. It's only been a few days. We have to exercise a little patience, I suppose."

"That's right. Logan, I..." But no, she told herself

again. Not now. It's not right to tell him something like this over the phone.

"What is it?" Concern threaded his voice. "Is something wrong?"

"No. Nothing. Nothing at all. I just… I'll be glad when you're home."

Softly he agreed, "So will I."

Jenna hung up feeling like a two-timer, a woman of questionable moral character, dishonest and bad. She could have killed Mack McGarrity. She muttered a few choice expletives under her breath.

And then, before reason could reassert itself, she got out the phone book and looked up the number of the Northern Empire Inn.

She dialed it quickly, and when the operator answered, she growled, "Mack McGarrity's room, please."

He picked up after the first ring. "McGarrity here." His voice, so deep and firm and resonant, vibrated along her nerves, sent a shiver moving just beneath the surface of the skin.

She could hear a television in the background, a man talking, then audience laughter. "Hello?" he said, impatient now, sounding like the old Mack, the oh, so busy Mack, the Mack who'd dragged her to New York City without bothering to get her input on the move—and then hardly had a spare moment for her once he got her there.

She opened her mouth, then shut it without making a sound. What was there to say that she hadn't already said?

She heard him draw in a breath. And then, in tender reproach, he whispered her name.

"Jenna…"

She lowered the handset and laid it oh so carefully back in its cradle.

Jenna didn't sleep well that night. She couldn't get comfortable in her own bed. And then, when she finally did drop off, she had a dream about Mack.

About making love with Mack.

In the dream, their lovemaking was every bit as beautiful, as sensual and sweet and soul shattering, as it had been in real life.

They lay on a white bed—the bed in the window of her shop, as a matter of fact. In the dream, though, the bed drifted in some warm and safe and hazy place. It floated, with Jenna and Mack naked upon it, in a kind of misty void.

Mack touched her, the way he used to touch her—in the beginning, when it was all so new and magical. When what he'd found with her was still enough to make him put aside temporarily the demons of ambition that drove him.

His eyes were the sky, blue turning cloudy. His hands, so warm and strong, moved over her body in a lazy, arousing dance. She moaned, and he kissed her, the deepest, longest, most sensual kiss she had ever known. It went on and on. She pressed herself closer to him and realized that he was already within her. There was that perfect, full sensation of joining.

Her eyes drooped closed. His kiss deepened even more. Impossible, that a kiss already so deep could continue to intensify. But it did. And they were moving together, sighing together, on the wide white bed in the middle of a warm and lovely nowhere.

Then all at once she was standing in the waiting room of a doctor's office, looking through the receptionist's window.

And it was Logan, not a receptionist, who stared back at her. "There's no cure for you, Jenna." His voice was icy cold. "I'm afraid your case is terminal."

She woke with a cry, sitting straight up in bed.

The next day Jenna looked in the phone book for the number of the attorney who had handled her divorce from Mack. It wasn't there. She remembered the address, so she drove by the attorney's office that evening, on the way home from Linen and Lace. But her lawyer had moved. The building was now occupied by a florist's shop.

Logan didn't call that night. Jenna felt guiltily grateful for that. As long as she didn't talk to him, she didn't have to keep asking herself if it was better to tell him the truth right now or to wait until she could tell him to his face.

Sunday, Linen and Lace opened at one in the afternoon. Jenna went out at a little after ten o'clock and bought bagels and cream cheese. Then she woke Lacey and the two of them sat in the breakfast nook, warm September sunlight pouring in the windows, drinking coffee and sharing an impromptu brunch.

Lacey talked a little about her stalled career dreams. She'd been living in L.A. for five years now. She shared a downtown loft—in a rather rough neighborhood that made Jenna nervous—with a friend, a fellow artist. Lacey painted every chance she got, and she was making connections, building a network of people who knew and liked her work. Every now and then she'd sell a painting. But as yet, her long string of jobs waiting tables and serving at private catered events were what paid the rent.

Jenna really did believe her sister had talent. And Lacey had come a long way from the troubled, rebellious teenager who'd once been known by her teachers as the Scourge of Meadow Valley High. Now Lacey really *cared* about something.

"You work hard," Jenna told her. "And you love what you do. You just keep working. Someday you'll get the recognition you deserve."

Lacey had what Jenna always thought of as a naughty angel's face—wide blue eyes, a lush, full mouth, a delicate nose and beautiful pale skin. She liked to wear tight-fitting tops and flowing, semitransparent skirts. To Jenna, she always seemed a cross between a rock star and a fairy princess.

Now the full mouth was stretched to a grin. "It's obvious why I come home—to hear you tell me that I'm bound to succeed."

"And you are. I *know* you are. Do you need money?"

"No, I do not. I'm managing just fine."

They shared a second bagel and Jenna poured them each more coffee.

Then Lacey asked, "So what's gone wrong in your life lately?"

Jenna tensed, but tried her best not to let Lacey see it. "What do you mean?" She hoped she sounded breezy. "Everything's fine."

Lacey leaned closer. "Come on. It's me. Your bad baby sister. I grew up spying on you, remember? I saw you get your first kiss."

This was news to Jenna. "You did not."

"I did. You kissed that redheaded boy, the one with all the freckles, whose ears stuck out. Chuckie…"

Jenna felt her cheeks coloring. "Oh, God. Chuckie Blevins."

"You were thirteen. And that Chuckie. He was some kisser. He slobbered all over you, and you wiped your mouth after. But in a very Jennalike way, so considerately, waiting until Chuckie wasn't looking."

"I can't believe you were *watching* that."

"You bet I was. It was probably the most exciting thing I ever saw you do." Lacey shoved a thick hank of curly blond hair back over her shoulder and sipped from her coffee cup. "And I still want an answer to my question. What's going on?"

"I don't—"

"Oh, stop it. *Something* is going on. You try to hide it, but you've got that worried, nervous look in those eyes of yours. It's the way you looked when you ran away from Mack McGarrity."

Jenna stiffened. "I beg your pardon. I did not—"

Lacey didn't even let her finish. "You did, too. Okay, okay. You called it a visit home. But you brought your cat with you, for heaven's sake. And you never did go back to New York. You bustled around here, inventing little cleaning and decorating projects to spiff up the house, acting busy but looking worried and sad, putting on fake smiles and trying to stay upbeat. But I could see. Anyone who cared about you could see. Something was very wrong."

"Well, my marriage was ending. Of course I was worried. And I didn't go back to New York because there was no point in going back. It was over between Mack and me."

"Jenna. I'm saying that you've seemed the same way for the last couple of days—not sad this time so much, but worried and really preoccupied. And I want to know what's bothering you."

Jenna looked at her sister for a long time, torn between the probable wisdom of keeping her own counsel and the real need to share her problem with someone she could trust.

Need won out. "Mack's in town."

Lacey set down her bagel without taking a bite of it. "You're joking. It's a joke, right?"

"No. It's no joke."

"In town? *Where* in town?"

"He's staying at the Northern Empire Inn."

"And he came to town to see *you?*"

"Yes."

"Does Dr. Do-Right know?"

"Lacey, I really wish you'd stop calling Logan Dr. Do-Right."

Lacey wrinkled her nose. "Sorry." Then she put on a contrite look. "Let me try again. Does *Logan* know?"

"I'm telling him as soon as he gets back from Seattle."

"Translation—you haven't told him yet." Lacey picked up her bagel again, looked at it, then dropped it for the second time. "I can't stand it. Talk. Tell me *everything.*"

"It's awful," Jenna warned. "It's embarrassing and unfair and just plain wrong. And if I thought I could get away with it, I'd do something life-threatening to Mack McGarrity."

"Just tell me what's going on."

So Jenna explained the whole mess to her sister.

At the end, Lacey asked, "Have you called your lawyer about it?"

Jenna sighed. "I don't have a lawyer, not as of this moment. The lawyer I did have has apparently closed up shop and moved away. He's not in the phone book anymore. And yesterday I drove by the address where he used to have his office. There's a florist shop there now."

"Great," Lacey remarked, in a tone that said it was anything but. "So you need a new lawyer."

"That's right. And I'll need a good one, I think. If I do end up having to divorce that man for the second time, he's promised me he'll think of a thousand ways to drag things out all over again."

"You know, he's always been kind of an SOB."

"You said it, I didn't."

"Maybe if you just hang tough, he'll give up."

"I keep hoping the same thing. But…" Jenna let a weary shrug finish the thought.

Lacey nodded. "Mack McGarrity is not the type who gives up."

"Exactly."

Lacey picked up her coffee mug and sipped. Then she set the mug down. "Can I ask you something?"

"Go ahead."

"Didn't you *notice* that you never got the final papers for your divorce?"

Jenna braced her elbows on the table and rubbed at her eyes. "It crossed my mind now and then. But you have to understand, it was *over*. We'd made an agreement. The rest felt like formalities. And I wasn't thinking about marrying anyone else then, so…"

Lacey was watching her way too closely. "Don't hate

me, but are you *really* sure it's over between you and
Mack?"

Jenna's answer was immediate. "Of course I am.
Why?".

"Well, there was just something so…powerful between the two of you. It's not the same with Dr. Do—
er, Logan."

Jenna knew she shouldn't ask, but she couldn't seem
to stop herself. "What do you mean, not the same?"

"Well, you and Logan are just perfect for each other,
on the surface. A couple of straight arrows who want
to raise a bunch of cute, happy kids. But there's something a little bit…" Lacey let the sentence trail off unfinished.

Jenna shifted in her chair impatiently. "What? A
little bit what?"

"I don't know. Lukewarm, I guess. Something kind
of tepid about the whole thing."

Jenna felt defensive—and tried not to let it show.
"Logan and I are both mature adults now. We know
what we want. If that seems lukewarm to you—"

Lacey put up a hand, palm out. "Look. Sorry. I'm
talking out of turn. Logan adores you. He always has."

Jenna easily read between the lines of what Lacey
had just said. When Lacey used words like *tepid* and
lukewarm, it wasn't Logan she was talking about.

Jenna shifted in her chair again. "There is a lot more
to making a marriage work than how much heat is gen-
erated."

"I realize that," Lacey said gently. "Honestly I do."
She reached across the table and wiggled her fingers.
"Come on. Put 'er there."

Jenna slid her hand into her sister's.

"So," Lacey said. "What do you plan to do now?"

Jenna groaned. "Leave the country?"

Lacey gave Jenna's hand a squeeze. "Come on. Seriously. What next?"

"Well, I'll see a lawyer on Monday, just to make certain of my options."

"And then?"

"If it turns out there's nothing I can do but give Mack his two weeks or divorce him all over again, I'm going to wait a while. Hang tough, as you put it. See if, just maybe, I can outlast him. I mean, eventually he has to get tired of hanging around here…doesn't he?"

"Hey, don't ask me. I'm only the little sister—and if he won't give up and give you the papers, then what?"

"What choice do I have? I'll start divorce proceedings. Again."

Lacey looked down at their joined hands. "What will you tell Logan?"

"The truth."

"When?"

Now Jenna was squeezing Lacey's hand. She teased, "For someone who has never liked Logan, you seem awfully worried about him all of a sudden."

Lacey pulled away. "What do you mean, I never liked Logan? Of course I like Logan. Just because he drives me insane with his endless and irritating advice on how I should run my life doesn't mean I don't care about him—and you haven't answered my question. When will you tell him?"

"As soon as he gets back from Seattle."

Jenna went to see a new lawyer on Monday and heard what she already knew. She could turn in the old papers, signed by both parties, and be eligible to re-marry in about six months. Or she could start the whole process all over again.

After she talked to the lawyer, she did nothing. After all, she told herself, that was what she had planned to do, see if she could wait Mack out.

Logan had arrived home too late on Sunday for them to get together. But Monday night they went out to dinner. Jenna planned to tell him about Mack then. But she didn't. She said nothing. She spent the meal asking him a thousand unnecessary questions about his trip and trying her best not to let him see how on edge she was.

Logan stopped in at the house for a while when he took her home. Lacey was there. Logan mentioned that he'd noticed an ad in the *Meadow Valley Sun.* The local art supply store needed a sales representative.

"Thanks, Doc," Lacey replied. "But I think I'd rather enter a convent. Or maybe hire myself out to a medical research lab somewhere. You know, as a human guinea pig for important experiments that could mean the end of cancer in our lifetime."

Logan let out a weary sigh. "Lacey, I'm not joking. It might turn out to be a good thing for you."

Lacey opened her mouth to utter more wisecracks, but Jenna caught her eye. Lacey smiled sweetly. "No, thanks, Doc. Really." A moment later she slipped from the room.

She reappeared as soon as Logan left.

"You didn't tell him, did you?" She was shaking her head.

"I just couldn't bear to."

"You'll have to. Eventually."

"I know. And I will. Eventually."

But not right now.

For right now, Jenna waited. Though she couldn't sleep at night and she was distracted in the daytime, she waited. And felt frustration and misery and a kind of righteous fury that Mack had put her in this untenable position in the first place.

She waited, hoping against hope that Mack would see how unreasonable and outlandish his ultimatum was. That she'd check the mailbox one evening and find the signed papers there—along with a short note of apology from Mack saying he regretted any pain he'd caused her and he was headed back to Key West.

She waited.

And she thought too much about Mack—so much that she found herself wishing more than anything that she could make herself *stop* thinking about him. She wished she could stop thinking about the ways he was the same as he used to be—and the ways he was different. Wished she could stop wondering about what he might be doing with himself, hanging out at the Northern Empire Inn with nothing to do but wait for her to call. She wished she could stop thinking about how she shouldn't be thinking about him and she was going to *stop* thinking about him—which only led her to think about him some more.

On Wednesday she and Logan met for lunch. He frowned at her across the table and said she seemed distracted lately. He wanted to know what was wrong.

She evaded. She thought, *this* will *all blow over. Mack will come to his senses and send me the papers and then Logan and I can laugh about how silly the whole thing was.*

Logan said, "Those papers haven't come from Florida yet, have they? Is that what's been on your mind?"

She gulped and admitted that the divorce papers *had* been on her mind, and that no, she didn't have them yet.

"Maybe you should call Mack McGarrity again."

Before she was forced to come up with a reply to that suggestion, the waiter miraculously appeared with their food. Once the waiter left, she exercised great care to move the conversation onto safer ground.

On Wednesday evening, as she was closing up the shop, Jenna thought she saw Mack across the street, just going into a store called Furniture By Hand. She stood at her own shop window for several minutes, waiting to see him come out of the other shop's door. He never emerged, at least not while she watched for him.

She wondered, was it really Mack? Or just someone who looked like him? Or worse, could it be her imagination working scarily overtime? It occurred to her that she couldn't even be sure that he was still in town.

That night she called the Northern Empire Inn for the second time. She asked for Mack McGarrity's room. And the clerk put her through.

He answered on the second ring that time. "McGarrity here."

She said, "I was hoping you might have come to your senses and gone home."

"No. I'm still here."

"This isn't right, Mack. It isn't fair."

She heard him draw in a breath. "It's only two weeks, Jenna."

"Give me those papers and go back to Florida where you belong."

"Not until you come with me."

She knew that the next thing she said would be shouted. So she hung up the phone, her nerves disgustingly aflutter.

She thought of those words her sister had used. *Lukewarm.* And *tepid.*

There was certainly nothing tepid about her response to Mack McGarrity.

But what about Logan? *Was* she lukewarm and tepid when it came to him?

Well, what if she was—just a little?

Maybe she liked it that way. Maybe she was mature enough now to appreciate a kinder, gentler sort of love.

Except…

Well, it *had* been beautiful with Mack. In bed. Beautiful and astonishing and utterly right.

And the truth was, she and Logan had never actually made love. Not in the complete sense of the word. Not in the consummated sense.

They'd agreed to wait until after the wedding.

And waiting had seemed good and right, up till now.

Up till Mack McGarrity had appeared in town.

Up until those dreams Jenna kept having now about the way it used to be with Mack. How Mack couldn't keep his hands off her and how she couldn't stay away from him.

How they *didn't* wait.

Maybe, she thought Wednesday night, after she hung up on Mack for the second time that week, she and Logan needed *not* to wait. Maybe she and Logan needed a night in each other's arms. A night to seal their bond in the most elemental of ways.

Yes. That might just be it. She needed to make love

with Logan in order to wipe out the memory of Mack's touch.

She shared her insight with Lacey on Thursday night.

Lacey blinked those big blue eyes. "Wait a minute. You're saying you and Dr. Do-Right have never...?"

"We were waiting." Jenna hated how prim she sounded. "Until the wedding. And stop calling him Dr. Do-Right."

Lacey nodded, a very unconvinced sort of nod. "Waiting. Right."

"People do wait, you know."

"I know."

"You're not acting as if you know."

"Well, I mean, it just took me by surprise, that's all. The thought of it, of you and—"

"Do not call him—"

"I won't. The thought of you and *Logan*..." Lacey's face was red.

"The thought of Logan and me what?"

"Well, you know. In bed. Making love. I never thought about that. But I guess that makes sense—that it would be hard for me to picture." Lacey laughed, a thoroughly irritating little titter of a laugh. "Because you've never done it, right?"

Jenna felt vaguely insulted. "You are not helping me out one bit here."

"I'm trying."

"Try harder."

"I will."

"Good. So?"

"So, in my humble opinion, if you really want to seal your bond with Logan, the first thing you ought to do is to tell him the truth. That Mack's taken a room at the Northern Empire Inn and he intends to stay there until you agree to go away with him."

"I am *not* going to go away with Mack."

"Don't tell me that, tell Logan."

"I will."

"When?"

"Tomorrow night, all right? Is that good enough for you?"

"Now is better. And don't look at me like that. You asked."

"Well, fine. All right. I'll call him right now, tell him I need to talk with him."

Lacey turned around and snared the phone off the breakfast nook wall. "Here you go."

Jenna took it—and then just sat there, holding it.

"What?" Lacey groaned. "All of a sudden you've forgotten his number?"

"Of course I haven't forgotten his number. I know his number."

"Hey. Look here. You've got him on auto dial."

"Lacey—"

But it was too late. Lacey had punched the button and Logan's phone was ringing.

"This is Dr. Severance."

"Uh. Hello."

"Jenna. Hello." As always, he sounded so happy to hear her voice. "What's up?"

"I wonder…" She hesitated.

Lacey mouthed the words, *Do it!*

Jenna made a face at her sister and then forced herself to go on. "Do you think you could come over here? There are a few things I need to talk to you about." Lacey gave her the high sign and a big, congratulatory grin.

Logan said, "Are you all right?"

"I'm fine. I just...really need to talk to you."

"I'll be over right away."

Chapter 4

Lacey decided to make herself scarce. As she went out the door, she advised, "Don't wait up—and don't you dare chicken out this time."

"I won't," Jenna replied, sounding a lot more confident than she felt.

Logan arrived five minutes later. Jenna led him to the back parlor, the big, comfortable room off the kitchen, where the family had always gathered. He sat on the roomy dark green convertible sofa and looked up at her, a worried frown creasing his brow. "This is about whatever's been bothering you for the past week, isn't it?"

She sat down beside him. "Yes."

He turned toward her, still frowning. In his somber expression she saw his concern for her. And his love. "You know that whatever it is, you can tell me, don't you?"

"I know. I just…"

"You know that I love you?"

"I do. And I love you." It was true. She did love him. But not in the way she had loved Mack McGarrity. And that did bother her. It bothered her terribly.

"Logan, I wonder…?"

"Yes?"

"Would you…kiss me? Really kiss me?"

He sat back from her a little. "Kiss you? I thought you were going to tell me—"

She put three fingers lightly against his lips to silence him. "I will. I'll tell you. I'll explain everything. Just…would you please kiss me first?"

His dark gaze scanned her face. "Kiss you."

"Yes. Please."

His expression softened a little, the worried frown fading. He slid an arm around her shoulder and gently, with the tip of a finger, tipped her mouth up to his.

Light as a breath, his lips met hers. His mouth was warm and soft and his big arms cradled her cherishingly.

She closed her eyes and tried to give herself fully to the act of kissing him, sliding her hands up his broad chest, allowing her lips to part, inviting him to deepen the kiss. His tongue slid into her mouth.

Jenna sighed. But she knew as the small, tender sound escaped her that it was a fake sigh, a forced sigh, an effort to convince herself—and Logan, too—that she was an eager participant in this.

Jenna closed her eyes tighter, kissed him back harder, tried to call up memories of when they'd been teenagers.

Teenagers necking in the front seat of his car.

It had been exciting then, hadn't it? She was certain it had.

But now wasn't then.

Between now and then, there had been Mack.

Mack.

That did it. Just the thought of his name.

Jenna shoved at Logan's chest.

Startled, Logan pulled away enough to look down at her. "What is it? What's wrong?"

He still had his arms around her. She felt trapped there, all wrong there. "Please. Let go."

He released her and sat back. "Jenna. What the hell is going on here?"

"I…I don't think I can marry you, Logan." She didn't know she was going to say it until after the words were out. And then, once she *had* said it, she stared at him, stunned at what she herself had just uttered.

Logan stared back at her, bewildered. And hurt. "Why not?"

She took his hand and looked into his face, right into his eyes. "You are such a good man. A *kind* man. A man who wants just what I want. A man I could always count on to be there when I needed him…"

"Then why can't you marry me?"

"Because this…you and me…it just isn't right for me."

His dark eyes were shining, a shine that very well might have come from unshed tears. Jenna watched his Adam's apple move as he swallowed, forcing down the emotions a man hesitates to reveal.

When he spoke, as always, he strove for calm and reason. "And how did you come to this realization?"

She looked away, and then back. And then, finally,

she made herself say it. "Mack's in town. He's refused to sign the divorce papers unless I spend two weeks with him first."

Logan swore under his breath. Then he asked, carefully, "How long has he been here?"

"A week."

"And you…didn't feel you could tell me?"

"I kept hoping he'd give up and go away. I'm furious with him, and I can't believe he's doing this and…I just wanted it to all be over before I said anything to you."

"But it's not over."

Jenna hitched in a tight breath. "No. It's not."

"You're talking about more than just the divorce papers, aren't you? You're talking about you and him."

Jenna wished with all her heart that she didn't have to answer that. But she knew that she did.

"I believed it was over, between Mack and me," she said. "I swear I did, or I never would have said yes when you asked me to marry you."

"But…?"

"But the minute I saw him again…" She shook her head. "I *don't* want to get back together with him. It could never work out. But there *is* unfinished business between Mack McGarrity and me. And I think I'm going to have to take care of it."

"Wait a minute. Don't tell me that you'll do what he wants you to do, that you'll actually go away with him!"

Jenna swallowed. "I… It's possible. I just might."

Logan held her hand more tightly, squeezing the fingers hard enough that she winced. "Jenna. Look what's going on here, look at the way he's maneuvering you. He's a manipulative SOB."

Gently Jenna pulled her hand free. "Lacey more or less called him the same thing."

"It looks like this is one situation where Lacey and I actually agree."

"You don't understand. You don't know him. He lost his parents when he was very young. He never had a real family. He grew up in foster homes. He had to scratch and scuffle for everything he ever got. When he wants something, he goes after it, any way he has to."

"And he's decided, after all this time, that he wants you?"

"I can't read his mind. But I do know there was a time when he and I shared something very special. He told me last Friday that he was trying to come to grips with what went wrong."

"He's chosen a hell of a way to go about it."

"As I said, it's the only way he knows."

Logan made a low noise in his throat. "Listen to you. Defending him."

She put her hand against the side of his face, longing to make him understand. "Logan. I have to do this."

Scowling, he ducked away from her touch. "I think it's time I had a nice long talk with that—"

"Please. Don't."

"Jenna. He's forced you into this."

"No. No, he hasn't. I don't *have* to go with him. I could divorce him all over again. It might take time, but it wouldn't take forever. If I go away with him, it will be because I choose to do it. For myself."

Logan looked at her piercingly. "You're sure?"

"I am." She slid the ring off her finger and held it out.

"Keep it," Logan said.

"No. That wouldn't be right."

Reluctantly he took it. A few minutes later, she walked him to the door.

And ten minutes after that, she was walking out herself. She got into her car and headed straight for the Northern Empire Inn. She knew the way. The inn was a Meadow Valley landmark, built over a century before.

She was lucky. She found a parking space near the front entrance. The fine old wood floors creaked a little under her feet as she strode through the foyer and up to the front desk.

"Mack McGarrity's room, please."

The desk clerk, who looked about twenty and had big brown eyes, smiled at her sweetly. "I'll ring his room and tell him he has a visitor. Your name, please?"

"Just tell me where his room is. I'll find it myself."

"Oh, I can't do that." The clerk's brown eyes had gone wider than before.

"And why not?"

"Well, I mean, it's…" Her smooth brow furrowed as she tried to think why. And then she remembered. She announced, with great pride, probably quoting from a training manual, "Because all of our guests have a reasonable expectation of privacy."

Mack McGarrity has no expectation of privacy at all, Jenna thought, *not right now, not when it comes to me….*

But of course, she didn't say that. The clerk was only following orders. "My name is Jenna Bravo. Tell him I'd like to come to his room."

"One moment, please."

The clerk turned to the antique switchboard behind

her and rang Mack's room. When she turned back, she was all smiles again. "Mr. McGarrity is expecting you."

"I'll bet he is," Jenna muttered to herself.

"Excuse me?"

"I said, I'll be so glad to see him. Which room is he in?"

"He's taken the East Bungalow. Go out that door there, across the back patio and take the trail that winds to your right."

The East Bungalow, nestled among the oaks well away from the main building, was a wood-frame structure, blue with white trim. It had a cute little white porch, complete with a rocker, a swing and planters under the front windows. The lights were on inside, spilling a golden glow out into the mild September night.

The door was wide-open and Mack was standing in the doorway—lounging, really, looking lazy and insolent and quite pleased with himself. As Jenna marched up the porch steps to confront him, he gave her a slow once-over with hooded eyes.

Her body responded to his glance as if he had touched her. A hot little shiver slid over her skin, a shiver of awareness, of sensual recognition.

He straightened from his slouch and folded his arms over his chest. "It's about time you showed up."

She paused on the threshold. He was blocking the doorway. "May I come in?"

"By all means." He stepped aside.

She entered warily, into a front sitting room decorated in Victorian style, with lace curtains at the windows, glass-shaded lamps and a sofa and love seat with carved claw-footed legs. Most of the furniture had been pushed against the wall to make room for two desks, set at right angles to each other. One desk had a laptop, a fax machine and telephone on it, the other a full-size computer, complete with mammoth monitor. At the moment, the monitor was running a screensaver of planets, stars and moons hurtling endlessly through deep space.

"Well," Jenna said. "I see you've been keeping busy this week."

He closed the door. "I like to keep an eye on how my stocks are performing."

"Oh. That's right. You take big chances. And they pay off."

He grinned. "Do you remember *everything* I said the other night?"

"I remember all the important parts. Like what I have to do to get those divorce papers out of you."

He went to where all the furniture was crammed against the wall and pulled the coffee table out enough that there was room to slide onto the sofa behind it. "Have a seat."

"No, thank you. I'm here to ask if, just maybe, you might have come to your senses and decided to behave like a decent human being."

He shrugged and sat down himself, plunking his long legs on top of the coffee table and laying his arms along the sofa's carved back. "Come on, Jenna. You know I can't do that. I'm a *lawyer,* after all."

She glared down at him, determined to communicate her cold contempt for him and the havoc he'd wreaked on her nice, well-ordered life.

But truthfully, she didn't feel cold. She felt…energized. After days of confusion and misery, she was taking charge of this situation. And it felt good.

"All right," she announced. "You can have your two weeks."

He gave her a quick salute by briefly dipping his golden head. "I'm pleased to hear you've come to see things my way."

"No. No, I have not come to see things your way. Not at all. I've just agreed to *do* things your way—up to a point."

"Up to what point?"

"I want to make a few of the decisions."

He studied the toes of the expensive hand-tooled boots he was wearing and asked in a suspicious tone, "What kind of decisions are you talking about?"

"The major kind. You know, the kind I somehow never got to make when we were together. Such as where we'll go and what we'll do."

He swung his feet to the floor, shoved the coffee table a little farther from the sofa and braced his elbows on his knees. "I thought we could—"

"Save it. You can tell me what *you* want to do later, because we'll do what *I* want to do first. That's fair, isn't it?"

"Fair?" He looked at her as if he didn't know the meaning of the word—which, of course, shouldn't have surprised her.

"Yes, fair. I get to decide where we go and what we do during the first week. The second week will be yours."

He leaned back into the couch cushions. "How generous of you."

"I'm glad you think so. You will pay for all of it."

He didn't seem terribly upset by that news, but he did remark, "Let me get this straight. *You* get to decide where we'll go—and *I* have to pay for it all?"

"I'm only deciding half of the time. And you're the one who started this, remember? You're the one who camped out here and wouldn't leave until I did what you wanted. Well, I'm doing what you wanted. And you can darn well pay for it. Besides, you can afford it."

He muttered something under his breath.

"What's that?"

"Nothing. All right, all right. I'll pay."

"And we will have separate rooms."

He grunted. "Why did I know you were going to say that?"

"Separate rooms, Mack."

He let out a big, fake sigh. "All right. Separate rooms." He was grinning again, a very irritating grin. "But nothing says you can't change your mind."

"I will not change my mind." She was truly proud of how firm she sounded.

He looked wistful. "We did have a great sex life. Remember?"

She did remember, all too well. She repeated, "I won't change my mind."

"Never say never."

"Do you understand? Separate rooms."

"Yeah. Right. I hear you loud and clear." He chuckled. "You've changed, Jenna. You're not the same sweet, gentle-natured girl I married."

"You're right. I'm not. And maybe you're having second thoughts about this. It's okay with me. Really. Just sign those papers and—"

"Not a chance. We're doing this."

"Then I'll need a few days, to take care of things at my store and make our travel reservations."

He shrugged. "Fine. Can you have it all handled by Monday?"

"Yes, I can."

"And where are we going on Monday, anyway?"

She hadn't decided yet. But if she told him that, he'd only start in about where *he* thought they should go. "Let me surprise you."

"I never much liked surprises."

"Too bad. I'll make all the arrangements for my week. You can reimburse me later."

"The arrangements for *what?*"

"Uh-uh. I told you. It's a surprise."

He gave her an oblique look. "Am I allowed one request?"

"That depends on what it is."

"I'd really prefer we didn't stay here in your hometown."

She was tempted to tell him that it was her week and if she decided to remain here, they would. But that would only have been pure orneriness. Truthfully, she didn't want to stay in Meadow Valley any more than Mack did. In Meadow Valley they'd constantly have to worry about running into familiar faces—like Logan, for instance.

"Don't worry," she said. "We're not staying here."

The slight crease between his brows smoothed out—and he came right back with more demands. "If we're flying, be damn sure you at least book first-class seats."

"First-class it is."

He leaned an elbow on the sofa arm and rested his fist against his mouth.

She did not like the way he was looking at her. "What?"

He let the fist drop. "I see you gave the good doctor back his engagement ring."

She glanced down at her left hand, thought of Logan again, felt a stab of mingled guilt and sadness. "Wasn't that what you wanted?"

"I wanted you to go away with me. Is that really so bad?" His eyes were softer now, more gray than blue.

That softness did it, made her answer him honestly. "Mack, it's not what you wanted, it's how you went about getting it."

He sat forward again. "If I'd come to you and asked you to give me two weeks before making our divorce final, what would you have said?"

There was only one answer to that question, and they both knew it. "No."

His eyes had that gleam in them, the one that said he'd made his point. "So. What choice did I have?"

"You had the choice of asking me, and then accepting my answer."

"The way I asked you to come back to me seven years ago?"

She looked at him and shook her head.

"What?" he said. "I did. I asked."

"You did not ask, Mack. You never asked. You *told*."

"I flew here from New York just to try to talk to you. To get you to see that I—"

"Oh, please. You fit in a flight between meetings. You took a cab from Sacramento International and when you got here, you made the cabby wait. You pounded on the door of my mother's house at nine-thirty at night, in a hurry as always, and ready with your demands. When I opened the door, you didn't *ask* me anything. You *told* me to get my things together and get out to that cab. You had a midnight flight back to LaGuardia for both of us. And an important meeting the next afternoon at two."

"I was trying to make a future for us, damn it."

"Mack. By then, there was no 'us' to make a future for."

"I realize that now. I should have spent more time with you. But as I remember, that meeting I had to get back for *was* an important one."

She gave a weary little laugh. "You know, Mack, in the entire time we were married, I don't think you ever had a meeting that wasn't important."

"I came to get you. I wanted you with me. *You* were always the most important thing in my damn life."

"Thing, Mack? *Thing?* I think you just hit on the operative word."

"You know what I mean. You *were* important to me."

"You had a very strange way of showing it—and the point is, when you came to get me then, you did not ask. You told."

"And you said no."

"That's right. I did. It was a major breakthrough for me."

He wasn't all that interested in her breakthrough. "You said no," he reiterated. "The same as you would have said no this time around, if I'd asked. Or if I'd told. So I didn't ask *or* tell. I used a little leverage."

"And now, for some reason, you're trying to convince me, or maybe yourself, that using 'leverage' is okay. And I'm telling you it's not. It's what you did.

And we'll make the best of it. But it is not okay. Got that?"

"Yeah. I'd say you've hammered it in pretty good." He leaned against the sofa arm and gave her the same kind of slow once-over he'd given her when she came up the porch steps. "And you really are meaner."

"I warned you."

"It's okay. I can take meaner. Now."

She didn't trust the warmth in his eyes, or the sudden velvety sweetness in his deep voice. She moved back a step. "I should go."

"Why?"

Her knees had started doing that ridiculous wobbly thing—and her heart kept up a steady, rapid boom-boom-boom inside her chest. "I said I'd spend two weeks with you. Beginning on Monday, and it's not Monday yet."

"Nothing like a head start, I always say." He stood slowly, not making any sudden moves. "Have you eaten? We could—"

"I ate hours ago."

He stepped around from behind the coffee table. "A drink, then. The bar is right there." He gestured at an armoire against the wall to her right. Then he started toward her.

"No." She backed up a second step. And a third. "No drink. No, thanks."

He kept on coming. "Jenna. Are you afraid of me?"

"I am not."

"I never hurt you, did I?"

"Of course not—not physically, anyway. But…"

He knew what she meant. "There are other kinds of hurt."

"That's right."

"You hurt me, too."

"Then we're even."

"Yeah. Sure. We're even." He backed her right up against the section of wall next to the door. "Your upper lip is quivering, just like it used to do whenever something really got to you."

"It's not a quiver. It's a nervous twitch."

"It's twitching, then. I really like your mouth. Did I ever tell you that?"

"Yes." She cleared her throat. "You did. Way back when." She was thinking, *Tell him to step aside. To move back. To get out of the way so that you can go.*

"It's not a full mouth, but it's so nice and wide and friendly—and then, there are those dimples on either side when you smile."

"I am not smiling now."

"I know." He sighed. She felt his breath, sweet and warm, across her cheek. "And you want me to get back, right?"

"That's right."

"Because you're leaving."

"I am."

"Because you already ate and you don't want a drink."

"Yes."

"Because the two weeks don't begin till Monday."

She nodded.

"And you don't believe in head starts."

His mouth was very close. She was staring at it, remembering what it felt like on hers, remembering, all at once, their first kiss.

They'd been standing by a door then, too. The door

to his apartment in L.A. It was after they'd gone out to eat Italian food, and then returned to his place for that last cup of coffee.

She'd told him she did have to go. And he had walked her the few steps to the door. And she'd said something about taking Byron with her.

And he had touched her then, cradling her face in both of his warm hands, raising her chin so she had to look right at him. "I don't want you to go," he whispered.

And then he kissed her. She cried out at the first touch of his lips on hers, not a loud cry, but an urgent one. Her mouth opened beneath his. To her, it felt like the opening of her very soul. From that instant, she knew: this was the man for her.

"Stay," he whispered against her parted lips....

Jenna blinked.

She was not in Mack's old L.A. apartment. She was in the East Bungalow at the Northern Empire Inn. And she was leaving.

Mack said, very softly, "Are you sure you don't want to—?"

"I am sure."

He took the crystal doorknob and gave it a turn. The chirping of crickets from outside grew louder and the cool evening air came in around them.

She said, "I'll call you, as soon as I make the reservations."

He was still looking at her mouth. "I'll be here."

The three words sent a dangerous thrill zinging through her. *I'll be here.* Oh, what she would have given to have heard him say those words years ago. To have heard him say them then—and mean them. To have had him truly with her when he said he would be, instead of always working, always busy, always preoc-cupied, far away from her even when he seemed to be close.

Mack saw the wishful look on her face. It gave him hope—enough that he suggested one last time, "Change your mind? Stay?"

She shook her head and went out into the night, through the grove of oaks, along the trail that led to the glowing lanterns strung along the back patio of the Northern Empire Inn.

Chapter 5

Saturday, Jenna decided where she and Mack would be going. She booked their flights and made a few other calls. She also briefed her clerks on their upgraded responsibilities while she would be gone.

Lacey agreed to stay in town for the two weeks. She'd keep an eye on the shop, look after the house and take care of Byron. She said she wasn't quite ready for the L.A. rat race yet, anyway.

She also said she could not believe that Jenna had agreed to run off with Mack McGarrity.

"I try not to think of it as 'running off,' Lace."

Lacey heaved a big sigh. "Poor Logan—but I do think it's the best thing, whatever happens with Mack. You were the right woman for Logan, but he was never quite the right man for you. I just hope he gets over it. And I wish he had more friends—a brother or something, someone he could really *talk* to about it."

Jenna, who felt terrible about Logan herself, couldn't resist remarking, "It would have been nice if you'd shown him this much sympathy when he and I were engaged."

"Why? He didn't need it then. He really is such an irritating man. But now, well, I just worry about him, you know? I guess I have to admit, I've developed a certain…fondness for him, over the years."

Jenna was worried about him, too. Which was why she suggested, "Maybe you could stop by and see him, in a few days. You know, just to make sure he's doing all right."

"Oh, great idea. That's exactly what he needs. Your bad baby sister showing up at his door."

"I think it would mean a lot to him. I think he cares about you, too."

That seemed to give Lacey pause. "You do?"

"Yes. I know he got on your nerves, always pushing you to move back to town and 'settle down.' But he did it because you matter to him, I'm sure of that."

"Well," Lacey said. "I'll think about it. Visiting him, I mean."

Jenna called Mack Saturday evening to tell him they were booked on a flight from Sacramento to Denver. Their plane would leave at ten on Monday morning.

"What's in Denver?" he demanded.

She considered dragging out the "surprise," since she didn't really want to listen to him groan over where she'd decided they were going. But then again, he might as well groan now as later.

She said, "Denver is where my cousin Cash is picking us up. He has a small plane. He'll fly us to Medicine Creek, Wyoming. We're staying at the Rising Sun, which you just may remember is the Bravo family ranch."

Mack was still stuck back there with her first sentence. "Wait a minute. You have a cousin named *Cash?*"

"I'm sure I mentioned him when we were married." Not that he would have been listening.

He said, "We're still married."

"Let's not get into that right now, please. Back to Cash. His real name is John, but everyone calls him Cash. He's my second cousin, actually. His grandfather was my grandfather's brother, on my father's side."

"Right."

Jenna knew what Mack's face would look like right then. His eyes would have that glazed-over look they always got when she started talking about the various members of her extended family.

"I've wanted to go to Wyoming for a long time, Mack. I even asked you once or twice to go with me, way back when."

It had been a dream of hers to visit Wyoming ever since that awful second year of their marriage, after the move to New York City. She'd felt so lonely, so far away from home, a small-town girl in a very big city with a husband who had no time for her.

She'd learned from her mother that she had family right there in New York: Austin Bravo, a first cousin once removed. His children were grown. He and his wife, Elaine, lived on the Upper East Side.

Mack was supposed to have met Elaine and Austin. But as usual, at the last minute some problem at the firm came up and he backed out of the dinner engagement that Jenna had arranged with them. Jenna went alone. And Austin and Elaine had told her all about the ranch in Wyoming, which had been in the Bravo family for five generations.

Mack started grumbling. "What's it like in Wyoming in September, anyway? I'll bet it's damn cold. And it's windy there, too, did you know? Nothing but wind and prairie and cattle, from what I've heard."

"Mack, we are going to spend *my* week at the foot of the rugged Bighorn Mountains, getting to know the Wyoming branch of my family. Another second cousin of mine, Zach Bravo, whose father, by the way, is Austin Bravo, the one you were supposed to have met when we—"

"Can we skip what I was supposed to have done all those years ago? Please?"

"Certainly. As I was saying, Zach runs the ranch. He's married, has two daughters and a new baby due about three months from now. They're looking forward to our visit."

"Jenna, the whole point of this two weeks is that we're spending some time alone. That's *A-L-O-N-E.* Meaning just you and me. As in, *No one else around.* How are we going to be alone with your second cousin and his wife and the kids and the—"

"We will have time alone. I promise you."

He asked, "How big is this house where your cousin and his family live?"

"Not quite big enough for us to have separate rooms, I'm afraid."

"How sad," he said smugly. "So you're saying we'll be sharing a room, after all?"

"No, I'm not saying that at all. As it turns out, there's

a smaller house a little way from the main house. The woman who lives there is away on some kind of trip, so that's where we'll be staying. Tess—that's Zach's wife, the one who's having a baby—said that house had more than one bedroom. So we're in luck."

He muttered something that was probably an expletive.

She said, "I've got everything arranged."

"Yeah. I can see that—and I guess I'd better pick you up at eight Monday morning, all right? That'll get us to the airport in Sacramento in plenty of time."

"Eight sounds perfect."

Jenna hung up feeling really good. She was in charge and she and Mack were going somewhere she'd always wanted to go.

But by Monday morning at eight-thirty, as she paced back and forth in the foyer with her suitcases waiting a few feet away, she was not feeling good. Not feeling good at all.

As she paced, Byron appeared, tiptoeing along the hall between the back parlor and the front door. He strolled up to her, sat down in her path and looked up expectantly. She bent and took him into her arms.

He purred. She vented.

"Déjà vu," she muttered. "That's French for 'I've been here before,' and I have, Byron. You know that I have." She scratched the cat behind an ear. "'Eight o'clock,' he said. 'I'll pick you up at eight.' Well, as usual with Mack McGarrity, eight o'clock has been and gone and Mack McGarrity is nowhere in sight."

Right then, the phone rang. "Great. Now we get the

excuses." She put Byron over her shoulder and stalked to the extension in the front parlor.

"What?" she barked into the mouthpiece.

"You're mad."

"You're right."

"Look. Something's come up, something completely unexpected and I—"

"Unexpected?" She tried not to shriek at him. "It's an hour's drive to the airport. Our plane takes off in—" she glanced at her watch "—eighty-three minutes. We don't have *time* for the unexpected right now."

"Listen. I'm on my way."

"You had to call to say you're on your way?"

"I know I'm late. I'm sorry. I wanted to let you know that I *am* coming over there. In fact, I'm here. Look out the window."

She did, and saw a silver-gray Lexus pulling up to the curb. Mack was behind the wheel, a cell phone at his ear. He waved at her.

She set down the phone and marched to the foyer, where Byron began to squirm to be let down. She bent and set him on the floor. He ran off down the hall. Then she turned to pull open the door.

Mack strode swiftly up the steps toward her, wearing faded blue jeans, a black T-shirt and a dark leather bomber jacket, looking like Steve McQueen in *The Great Escape,* ready for anything and so handsome it hurt. Funny, she thought, he never used to wear blue jeans back when. Then, he wore expensive suits and designer ties—even at first, when he couldn't afford them. Apparently now that success was his, he no longer felt the pressing need to dress for it.

She stepped back and gestured him over the threshold, turning immediately for her suitcases. "Come on. Let's get these out to the car and—"

"Jenna."

She did not like the way he said her name. Slowly, she turned back to him. He had both hands stuck in the pockets of that gorgeous leather jacket and a very guilty expression on his face. That was when she knew what he was going to say next.

She said it for him. "You're backing out."

"Jenna, I—"

She went to the door and shut it. Then she planted both fists on her hips. "Just say it. You're not going."

"There's a…crisis. I'm sorry. I don't like it. But I'm going to have to put off our two weeks together."

"A crisis."

"Yes." He spoke very quietly, too quietly, in fact. "A crisis. Something I just can't put off dealing with."

"A meeting, right? A really terribly un avoidably *important* meeting. Am I right?"

"No. You're not." His voice rose in volume. "It's not a damn meeting."

"Stop shouting," she said. "You'll wake up my sister."

His mouth became a flat line and he muttered, "Sorry," but not as if he really meant it.

"Well," she said, making no effort at all to mask her sarcasm. "I suppose I should think of this as progress. At least you're telling me in person that you can't do what you said you'd do. The old Mack would have gone ahead and told me over the phone."

"You may not believe me, but this *is* important. I'm flying to Long Beach right away and—"

"Long Beach? Long Beach, California?"

"Right. And—"

"What's in Long Beach?"

He didn't answer, just went on with what he'd been saying before. "The minute this situation is handled, I'll call you and we can—"

"What *situation?*"

"*This* situation."

"Mack. I am exerting great effort not to start shouting at you. You could help me a little here. You could tell me what the problem is. You could tell me *why* you're backing out on me."

"I'm not backing out on—"

"What *is* the problem?"

He glared at her, then he sucked in a big breath and raked his hand back over his hair. "It's not a good idea, I think, to go into it now. If you'll just wait until I've—"

"Wait? You want me to *wait?*"

"Yeah, but only until I've taken care of this thing and we have a little time to—"

"Stop. Stop right there." She held up her left hand and wiggled the fingers at him. "Notice. No engagement ring. Because of you, I have broken up with a wonderful man who loved me with all of his heart."

Mack made a low noise in his throat. "What? You expect me to feel guilty about that? Well, I don't. Not one damn bit. It was a wise move on your part. You're not ready to marry the good doctor right now. It wouldn't be good for you, and it certainly wouldn't be good for him to marry another man's wife. You need—"

"Do not tell me what I need, Mack McGarrity. Listen to what *I* am telling *you.* You wanted two weeks. I am giving you two weeks. And those two weeks are starting *right now.*"

"Jenna, I'm trying to tell you that I—"

"Stop talking. Listen. If the two weeks do not start now, they are not going to start at all, because I will do what I threatened to do when you first proposed this crazy scheme of yours. I'll divorce you all over again."

"Jenna. That's foolish. You don't want to do that."

"That's another thing I never could stand—the way you always thought you knew what I wanted. Well, you don't know what I want. *I* know what I want. And if you listen, I'll tell you. I want our two weeks to start right now. I'm ready to start right now, ready to get it over with. I don't want to wait around until *you* decide *you're* ready. I've been there and done that back when I lived with you."

"This is hopeless," he said. "You just will not listen. I keep trying to tell you that doing it now is not possible."

"Yes, it is possible. Because I'm willing to compromise a little."

"Compromise. I don't like that word."

"That's only because you have never done it in your life. But you're going to get your chance now. This is my offer. Your week will come first. We can spend it doing whatever it is you just *have* to fly to Southern California to do."

"That's a bad idea."

"Take it or leave it."

"No. Jenna. What I have to do right now isn't what I had in mind for my week at all. I wanted us to get away together, to be alone someplace private, someplace beautiful. I was hoping—"

"Stop trying to soften me up. You can't. I've been through it all with you before. We're going to Long

Beach for this emergency of yours—or we aren't going anywhere."

He scraped a hand through his hair again, stared down at his boots and shook his head.

"I mean it, Mack. We start today, or we never start at all."

"Jenna…"

"And right now, before we begin, you are going to tell me what this emergency is."

"Damn it, Jenna."

"Now."

"All right," he said—and then he looked away.

She waited for a count of ten and then demanded, "Mack. Tell me."

He turned to her, glaring. "My mother is sick. They believe that she's dying."

Jenna was certain she hadn't heard him correctly. "Excuse me. I could have sworn you just said—"

"I did." He said it again. "My mother is dying."

"But…how could that be? You don't have a mother. Do you?"

Chapter 6

Mack felt like an idiot as he was forced to confess, "Yes, Jenna. I do have a mother." He couldn't believe she'd kept after him until she'd made him tell her. The old Jenna would never have been so determined.

Oh, where had the old Jenna gone?

The new Jenna was shaking her head. "But you always said… You always led me to believe that you had no family, that you'd been raised in foster homes."

"I *was* raised in foster homes—mostly, anyway." Damn, he did not want to go into all this now. "Look. It's complicated. It's one of the things I thought we'd be talking about during our two weeks."

"Well. I guess you thought right. We will be talking about this mother you never said you had during our two weeks, which are starting now. I assume you've already set up a flight?"

"I have a plane waiting at Sacramento Executive Airport. And we need to get on it ASAP." He picked up her two suitcases, leaving the small overnight case for her to deal with.

She followed behind him, not arguing for once, as he went out the door and down the porch steps.

On the drive to Sacramento, Jenna used Mack's cell phone to call her family in Wyoming and tell them that their visit had been postponed. She also called the airline to say they wouldn't be making the Denver flight.

The private plane, a twelve-seater, was ready for takeoff when they got to the airport. The pilot loaded their baggage as Jenna and Mack settled into the passenger cabin, which was empty save for the two of them.

As soon as they were in the air, she turned to Mack. "Okay. Tell me about the mother you never said you had."

Mack had taken the window seat. He stared out over the wing at Sacramento's considerable urban sprawl. "Do you know that one in eight Americans lives in the state of California? Pretty incredible, huh?"

"Mack." Her voice was gentle.

It hurt, somehow. That gentleness. Hurt much more than all the hard accusations she'd hurled at him just about every time they'd spoken over the past week and a half. It hurt because it reminded him of the old Jenna. And of all he'd lost when he lost her.

Of all it was very possible he could never get back.

She wasn't the same.

But then, neither was he.

And the attraction was still there. That, he was sure

of. For him and for her, too, no matter how hard she tried to hide it.

In the end, it hadn't worked the way they were. Maybe it would turn out that they were both different enough in the right kind of way. Maybe a new beginning would be possible.

Then again, maybe he was whistling in the dark.

"Mack?"

He turned to look into the face that he'd never been able to forget, the face that had, on more occasions than he would ever be willing to admit, appeared in his dreams. "I didn't lie to you, not exactly."

The dimples he'd always loved showed faintly at the sides of that wide mouth of hers. "You lied only by omission."

"That's right."

"So. Now's the time to tell me what you left out."

He didn't know quite where to begin.

In that gentle, old-Jenna voice, she prompted, "You told me that your father died when you were six."

"That's right. And that was the truth."

"Somehow, I got the idea that your mother died shortly after."

"Maybe because that was what I wanted you to think. But my mother didn't die. She is alive—or she was a few hours ago. And I...have two sisters." Hazel eyes widened the tiniest bit in shock at that news. He added, feeling just a little guilty, "I never told you that, either, about my sisters, did I?"

"No, Mack. You never did."

"Bridget and Claire. They were eight and four when my father died."

"You also never told me...how your father died."

"He was killed in a convenience-store holdup. He was the poor chump behind the counter. They were young, my parents. They didn't have much."

"That must have been tough on your mother."

"That's right. She didn't know what to do. She couldn't support us by herself. She put the three of us into foster care and got a job as a secretary in a small employment agency. For a while, she would come and visit us all the time."

Jenna touched the back of his hand. Mack felt that touch to the center of himself. But it must have been an unconscious gesture, one she instantly regretted, because she jerked her hand back within seconds after she made contact.

She asked, "What do you mean, she visited for a while?"

"I mean that the visits tapered off. Bridget and Claire and I were all in different foster homes by the time I was seven. And it was around that time that my mother started coming less and less often to see me. She came on my eighth birthday, I remember that. It was the last time."

"You mean, after that you never saw her again?"

The disbelief on Jenna's face made him smile. He remembered her mother, Margaret, who had been tall and capable, with a wide smile a lot like Jenna's. Jenna's father had died when Jenna was—what?—fifteen or sixteen, Mack was pretty sure. He was also sure that it had never occurred to Jenna's mom to put her children in foster care, let alone to relinquish all claim to them.

But then again, Jenna's father had been a successful insurance salesman and Jenna's mother had run the office for a title company. No doubt there had been a big life insurance policy and sufficient money coming in that Jenna's mother never had to worry all that much about where her family's next meal would come from.

Mack shrugged. "My mother came to see me on my eighth birthday, and that was it."

"But why? Why would she do that, desert you like that?"

"It turned out that she wanted to marry her boss—and she never managed to tell him about the kids she'd farmed out. When he proposed, she put us up for adoption, giving up all claim to us, along with any responsibility for our care."

"They told you that when you were a child?"

"No. They only said, as gently as they could, that my mother couldn't take care of me anymore and I had become a ward of the court. I found out why later, after the class-action suit."

"Why not until then?"

Mack looked out the window again. The steady drone of the engines filled the cabin, and high white clouds rose up like towers of cotton in the distance.

"Mack."

He looked at her again then. "All those years when I was growing up in other people's houses, and later, when I was slaving away at college, when I met you...I just wanted to forget about her. Even though I didn't have the facts then, I knew that she had dumped me, that she had tossed me and my sisters overboard like so much extra baggage in a sinking boat."

Right then, Jenna ached for him. And maybe she understood him a little better than before. Was that a good thing? She wasn't sure. She felt such conflicting

urges when it came to Mack, not the least among them
the compelling need to guard her heart against the kind
of damage he had inflicted on it before.

He said, "All my life I wanted money. Lots of it. I
guess it's a classic situation. I thought money would
protect me against the kinds of losses I suffered as a
kid. Then I got what I wanted. I had money. And not
much else."

Jenna's heart contracted. *Not much else.* She supposed
that was true, in a way. He didn't have his family—his
mother or his sisters. And he no longer had a wife.

He went on, "So I hired investigators to help me find
out what had happened to my past."

"They tracked down your mother?"

He nodded. "I went to Long Beach, where she lives
now, and I contacted her. She agreed to meet me in the
lobby of my hotel."

"How long ago was this?"

"Two years. She was… She looked so small to me.
And kind of faded and tired. And so damn sad. She
cried, and she smoked cigarette after cigarette. And I
kept thinking I should put my arm around her or something, but I couldn't quite make myself touch her. She
said that she never had managed to tell her husband
about us—Bridget and Claire and me—and she just
didn't know how she was going to be able to bring herself to tell him then, either."

Mack let out a long breath. "It's strange. In my mind,
over the years, I had made her into a kind of monster, a
damn evil bitch who had dumped her own children. But
looking at her then, I only felt sorry for her. She said
she knew it was terrible of her, that if I didn't hate her

already, I would when she asked what she was going to ask of me."

Jenna had a good idea what that must have been. "She still didn't want to tell her husband about you."

"That's right."

"And what did you say when she asked you not to tell him?"

"I said all right."

Jenna knew then, if she'd ever really forgotten, why she had loved this man. "Oh, Mack."

"Well." His voice was gruff. "What the hell else was I going to say? That I hated her guts and never wanted to see her again?"

"Some men might have said exactly that."

"No," he said. "No sense in that. I pretty much knew where I stood with her when I went looking for her."

"And since then?"

His mouth curved in a half smile. "I've kept in touch with her. I set her up with a P.O. box, so I could write to her and she wouldn't have to worry about her husband finding out. And she sends me stuff."

"Stuff?"

He looked embarrassed. "Stuff. You know, ugly ties for my birthday. Socks at Christmas. She's got a thing for those cheese-and-salami gift packs. You know, they come in a wooden box with a trademark branded into the lid. Inside, there's lots of fake green Easter-basket grass and different kinds of cheddar and smoked sausage—I get a lot of those."

Jenna's throat burned a little with the sudden pressure of tears. But she knew that Mack McGarrity had never been a man to accept a woman's pity. She swallowed the tears down and tried to speak lightly. "Oh, Mack. Cheddar and smoked sausage?"

"That's right. I tried to…help her out a little."

"Give her money, you mean?"

He nodded. "She wouldn't take it. She said that she and her husband were doing fine. She didn't need anything from me. She just wanted a letter now and then, and a place to send the salami and cheese."

Jenna had more questions. "Has she been ill for a while now?"

"Not that she told me about."

"But you said she was sick."

"A heart attack, pretty much out of the blue. She's only fifty-two. I picked up my messages this morning and there was one from her husband. I managed to reach him at the hospital. He told me that the prognosis isn't good and that she's asked to see me."

There was a positive note here. Jenna pounced on it. "Her husband, you said? Her husband was the one who called?"

"That's right. His name is Alec. Alec Telford. Seemed like a decent enough guy."

Jenna repeated the name. "Alec. And your mother… her name is Doreen, right?"

He looked vaguely surprised. "You remembered."

How could I forget? she thought. He had told her so little about his family. Every detail she'd squeezed out of him had been information to treasure. "I believe that you also told me her maiden name was Henderson."

He chuckled, but without much humor. "It looks like you've got all the facts."

She grunted at that one. "Hardly. And what I'm getting at here is that, since Alec was the one who called you, it looks as if Doreen did finally tell him the truth, right?"

"I guess we could logically assume that." He turned toward the window again. She knew he was hoping he'd answered enough questions for a while.

But she had one more she just couldn't hold back. "What about your sisters, Bridget and Claire? Did you find them, too?"

He turned to her with obvious reluctance and gave her his best lawyer's look. "And if I did?"

"Mack. Don't be like that. Just tell me. Did you find them?"

"Yes, I found them."

"And?"

"Jenna. Enough."

"No. Come on. I want to know about them."

"Oh, all right. Bridget's married. She and her husband have three kids. She lives in Oregon. And Claire is married, too. No kids yet, though. She teaches high school in Sacramento. From what my sources told me, both women are doing just fine."

"Sacramento? Did you stop in to see Claire, then, on your way to Meadow Valley?"

"No."

"But why not?"

"Jenna…"

"Oh, Mack, come on. I just want to know what your sisters are like."

"From the reports I got, they're nice, middle-class women with ordinary lives. But I can't say for sure. I've never talked to them."

She frowned, confused. "But why not? You went

to all the trouble of finding them. It seems to me that meeting them would be the next logical step."

"After what happened with my mother, it occurred to me that maybe they wouldn't appreciate my popping into their lives out of nowhere."

That was a phony excuse if Jenna had ever heard one. "But—"

"Jenna. Let it go, all right? I haven't contacted my sisters, and I won't be contacting them. I know they're okay and that's enough for me." He turned to the window once more and stared out, as if the sight of rearing clouds and the rolling, dry mountains far below utterly fascinated him.

At the hospital they asked at the front desk for Doreen Telford's room. The clerk gave them some mumbo jumbo about critical care and asked them to take a seat. Someone would be down to speak with them shortly.

Mack didn't like the sound of that. "What's wrong? Is she worse?"

"Sir, if you'll just have a seat, as I said, someone will—"

"I know what you said. And I asked if my mother's gotten worse."

"Sir, I—"

Jenna cut in then, taking Mack by the arm. "All right. We'll be right over there." She tugged on Mack's arm. "Come on. We can wait a few minutes. It's not the end of the world."

Mack glared down at her, but he did allow her to lead him over to a black leather bench against the adjacent wall. When they reached the seat, she pulled him down beside her.

"Something must be wrong," he said. He felt strange, uncomfortable in his own skin. And his stomach had knotted up. "I didn't like the look on that clerk's face."

Jenna patted his arm. "It's all right. Just relax. She said it would only be a few minutes."

In spite of the dread that tightened his gut, Mack almost smiled. Ever since he'd walked into her shop, ten days ago now, she'd made it painfully clear he was to keep hands-off. Never consciously had she touched him. On the plane, when she'd forgotten herself for a moment and reached out, she'd yanked her hand back so fast he could almost have missed the fact that she'd reached out at all.

So maybe this was a step in the right direction. She had her arm in his and she was holding on to him with her other hand.

All right, it was mostly to keep him from jumping up and laying into the admissions clerk. But she *was* holding on. And it felt damn good.

He endured the next ten minutes mostly because she *kept* holding on. He held on right back, even pushing it so far as to twine his fingers with hers—a move she allowed, though she stiffened a little at first and sent him a suspicious glance.

But then she relaxed. She held on to him and let him hold on to her. After all, it was the kind of grim situation when a man most needs a woman's touch.

Staring bleakly out over the reception area, Mack spotted the tall, stoop-shouldered man when he emerged from the hall to the elevators. The man wore a wrinkled short-sleeved dress shirt, dark slacks and black shoes. He had thinning gray hair and a certain look on his face: the glazed, rather numb stare of a man who has just taken a huge, unbearable blow and has yet even to begin dealing with it. A man in those first blank moments of pure shock.

Mack knew. It was his stepfather, Alec Telford. And he knew what the look on his stepfather's face meant.

He'd be getting no more boxes of salami and cheese in the mail. His mother was dead.

Chapter 7

The man Mack knew to be Alec Telford went to the admissions desk and spoke briefly with the clerk. The woman said something in reply, her gaze sliding over to where Mack and Jenna sat against the wall.

The tall, dazed fellow turned and came toward them.

Mack heard Jenna's voice, soft and cautious, in his ear. "Do you think that might be—"

"Yes." Mack let go of her hand. "I do." They stood at the same time.

The man stopped a few feet from them. "I... Hello, I'm..." He blinked, his kind brown eyes going more vacant than before, as if he couldn't quite manage to call up his own name. "Alec," he said at last. "Call me Alec." He made a brave effort at a smile, one that stretched his mouth into a pained grimace.

Jenna said, "Mr., er, Alec, maybe you ought to sit down."

The brown eyes blinked again. "Sit? No, I don't think so." He turned resolutely toward Mack and held out his hand. "You're Mack. Dory's..." He gulped, his eyes going watery. Then he blinked again. "You're Doreen's boy." He extended a hand.

"Yes. I'm Mack McGarrity." Mack held out his own hand. They shook.

Alec leaned toward Mack. "I'm so sorry to tell you this, but Doreen... She's gone. It happened just..." He blinked some more and then sent his vacant gaze wandering the room.

Finally he found what he sought: a clock, on the wall above the admission desk. "Just an hour ago. An hour and five minutes, actually. I was sitting with her. And she opened her eyes. She said, 'My arm hurts, Al. My arm really hurts.' And then...all those machines they had her hooked up to, those machines started beeping. Nurses and doctors came racing in. They did all they could, but they couldn't save her. She...she's gone now."

"Come on," Jenna said. "Come on, Alec. You sit down right here." She took the older man by the shoulders and guided him to the bench. Mack knew a moment of stark gratitude that she had forced him to bring her here.

Alec Telford let his head drop back against the wall and looked up at Mack and Jenna. "I...I'm sorry." He was frowning at Jenna. "You are...?"

She gave him one of those smiles that haunted Mack's dreams, wide and tender and achingly sweet. "Jenna. Jenna Bravo. I'm Mack's, um, friend."

Mack resisted the urge to jump in, to correct her, to insist, "She's Jenna *McGarrity*. And she is my wife."

Alec Telford, who had just lost his own wife, wouldn't give a damn anyway at that point.

"Well," Alec said, "nice to meet you, Jenna."

Jenna's beautiful smile got even wider. "Nice to meet you, too."

The older man tried to pull himself a little straighter. "I meant to…do better at this. I wanted to…" His sentence wandered off into silence.

"It's all right," said Jenna. "You're doing wonderfully. Really."

Mack took his cue from her. "Yes. Uh. Thank you. For coming down yourself to tell me."

"I… Well, it was the least I could do." The older man closed his eyes, licked his dry lips.

Jenna started moving away. Mack sent her a frantic look.

"Back in a jiff," she said, and headed across the room.

"So many…things to deal with," Alec Telford said. "I don't seem to be handling it very well."

"You're doing fine," Mack said automatically, watching Jenna as she went to the water cooler in the corner and filled a paper cup. "It's a big shock."

"You resemble her," Alec Telford said. Mack turned back to the man on the bench, who was staring at him with a sort of musing intensity that Mack found unsettling. "Not in size, of course. She was so small. But… the shape of the face. And the eyes. Those blue-gray eyes…"

My mother, Mack thought. *He's saying I look like my mother. What the hell should I say in response?* "Yes, I… Well, I…" God. Jenna needed to get back here. She needed to get back here right now.

And then miraculously, there she was, the filled paper cup in her hand. "Here, Alec. Some water, maybe...?"

"Oh. Thank you." Alec took the cup and drank it in one swallow—so of course Jenna had to trot right back to the cooler and get him more. Fortunately, while she was gone that time, Alec didn't feel the need to start in again about how much Mack looked like his mother.

Once he'd had his second cup of water, Alec pushed himself from the bench. "Well. I can't sit forever, now, can I? I admit, I've been sitting upstairs, since they... took her away. Just sitting there, thinking that I should get busy. And then they told me you had arrived, Mack. And so I..." He paused, closed his eyes, took in a breath. "I do believe I am babbling," he said.

"Alec." Jenna laid her hand on his thin, heavily veined arm. "Alec, is there anyone here with you, to help you?"

"Help me? No. No, I've...it's always pretty much been just Dory and me. But I'm...quite capable, really. I can manage. No problem." He blinked, turned to Mack. "Tonight. Could you come to the house, do you think? There are a few things Dory wanted you to have. You have the address?"

Mack nodded.

"And the phone number?"

"Yeah."

"About eight?"

"Sure."

"Good, then—oh. Wait. Where are you staying? I probably ought to know, just in case there's something I—"

Jenna cut in then. "Alec, we can deal with all this

later. Mack and I aren't going anywhere now. We're staying right here, with you, to help you."

Mack almost said, "We are?" But he shut his mouth over the words just in time.

Alec blinked some more. "Oh, no. I couldn't ask you. I can manage. Honestly, I—"

"Of course you can manage," Jenna said. "But there's no reason you have to manage, not all alone, anyway."

"You're...you're sure?"

Mack didn't think he'd ever seen anything so heartbreaking as the sheer relief on his stepfather's face when Jenna replied, "We're positive. We're staying with you."

They spent the rest of the day taking care of the thousand and one things that require attention when someone dies.

They found a funeral home. They contacted Alec and Doreen's insurance agent, settled up with the hospital and removed Doreen's few personal items from her room there.

Alec had a widowed sister, Lois Nettleby, who lived in Phoenix.

"I suppose I'd better call her," Alec said absently. "She and Dory weren't real close, but I think she'd want to know."

Jenna encouraged him. "Call her right now."

So he did. Lois promised she'd be on the first flight she could find.

Then they drove to the funeral home in the Lincoln that Mack had rented. There they chose a casket and set the funeral date: Friday, in the afternoon. Alec already had a place to bury his wife.

"We bought our cemetery plot two years ago," he said. "It was mostly for me, of course. She's thirteen years younger than I am…" He paused, swallowed. "Excuse me. I mean, she *was* thirteen years younger. We just… We never imagined that she'd be the first to go."

Jenna put her arm around his narrow shoulders. Mack watched from a few feet away, marveling, as he'd been doing for hours, at the ease and grace with which she soothed a virtual stranger's grief.

She whispered something in Alec's ear, too low for Mack to make out the words. Something reassuring, apparently, because Alec nodded and said, "Thank you, Jenna. I appreciate that."

When they were through at the funeral home, they returned to the hospital, where Alec got his car. Jenna rode with him to his house and Mack followed in the Lincoln.

The house was ranch-style, a reverse floor plan, with the kitchen toward the front. Alec took the mail from the mailbox before he unlocked the door.

Inside, the curtains were drawn and the stale air smelled faintly of cigarettes. Alec trudged to the kitchen and tossed the mail onto the table, adding to the pile already waiting there. The phone on the wall above the counter rang. Alec picked it up, said hello and then, "Yes. All right. Six-fifteen. We'll be there to meet you."

He hung up. "That was Lois. She's coming into John Wayne Airport at six-fifteen." A half-empty carton of cigarettes stood on the counter, near his elbow. Alec shook his head at them. "Dory…" It came out sounding suspiciously like a sob. But then he collected himself, and spoke with strictest self-control. "She never would quit." He grabbed the carton and threw it in the trash.

After that, he didn't seem to know what to do with himself.

But Jenna knew. "We need to make some calls, Alec. People will want to know what's happened, where to send flowers, what time the funeral will be."

At first, Alec protested that there was no one to call. But Jenna had him get out Doreen's address book. As he looked through the names and addresses, he found that there were several people who would want to be notified.

"Would you like me to call them?" Jenna offered.

"No. No, I think it's something that I ought to do myself."

As Alec made the calls, Mack decided he was getting pretty tired of feeling useless. He dug around in the cupboards and came up with stuff to make sandwiches. Standing side by side at the kitchen counter, he and Jenna put them together.

My mother's kitchen, Mack thought as he squirted mustard from a squeeze bottle onto slices of bread. *My mother's kitchen. Who would have thought I'd ever be here?*

An African violet in a glazed pot sat on the windowsill, surrounded by a large number of small ceramic animals: cats, dogs, horses, frogs...

A stunning flash of memory hit him: the kitchen window, in the house they'd lived in before his father died, the same—or at least, much the same—tiny animals arranged with care along the sill.

"Mackie..." His mother's voice. *"See, Mackie? A*

kitty and a doggy, a pony and parrot...no, no. Very
careful. They're fragile, Mackie. They could break...."

Mack closed his eyes, breathed in through his nose
as it struck him. What memories he had of her were all
he would ever have.

He wondered why that should hurt so much. It wasn't
as if he'd expected there to be more.

Jenna was rinsing lettuce in the sink. He glanced
over at her and she gave him one of her gorgeous
smiles. "Okay?" she asked softly.

He realized he did feel better. "Yeah. I'm okay."

They ate the sandwiches. Then it was time to head
for the airport in Orange County. Lois Nettleby's flight
got in right on time. Alec spotted her and waved as she
came down the exit ramp. She waved back, a pleasantly
stout woman with a deep tan and friendly wrinkles fan-
ning out from her dark eyes.

They drove Lois and Alec back to the house. By
then, it was after eight. Alec mentioned again the mementos he had for Mack, then added, "But I guess
there's no rush about them. We can take care of them
tomorrow. Could you come by in the morning, do you
think? Say, around ten?"

Mack said that he'd be there. He thought that dealing
with them tomorrow—whatever "they" were—sounded
like a great idea. Alec looked dead on his feet. And
Mack himself wanted a stiff drink, a long hot shower
and a king-size bed—preferably with Jenna in it.

And all right. Maybe he wouldn't get Jenna in his
bed tonight. But there was nothing in the agreement
he'd made with her that said he wasn't allowed to hope.

During their flight, he'd called and booked rooms

at a good hotel on Ocean Avenue. The fact that it was a Monday in late September worked in his favor. He'd had no problem getting a two-bedroom, two-bath suite with a big living area between.

They entered the suite through the little foyer that opened onto the living-dining room. Jenna stepped over the threshold with great caution and then stood looking at him with narrowed eyes.

He took off his jacket and tossed it over a nearby chair. "That look you're giving me shows a total lack of trust." He did his best to sound injured.

She wasn't buying. "We agreed. Separate rooms."

He marched over and opened a door. "Notice. A bedroom, complete with its own bath. See that door over there? You'll find the same thing if you open it."

Before she could comment, there was a tap on the entry door.

The bellhop. They waited as he distributed bags to their separate rooms, then showed off the wet bar and the refrigerator full of snacks and cold drinks. Finally he drew the curtains, revealing a balcony and a really splendid view of Long Beach Harbor at night. He pointed out Catalina Island, and a spur of land to the west where the *Queen Mary* was forever moored.

"If there's anything else I can get you, just buzz the concierge," he said. Mack produced a generous tip. With a blinding smile, the bellhop departed.

Mack and Jenna were left alone again, regarding each other.

Mack spoke first. "You were terrific today," he said. "Thank you."

She acknowledged his thanks with a slight dip of her head, then went to the glass door that looked out on the dark ocean, on the gleaming harbor lights. "It's important, I think, when you lose someone you love, to have people around you, people to help. I was glad we could do that for Alec." She took her gaze from the night and focused on him. "He's a very nice man."

"Yes," Mack said. It seemed a woefully inadequate response, but he had no better right then.

"Mack?"

"What?"

"I'm sorry. That she's gone."

For some reason, he had to look away.

She came toward him and stopped just a few inches away. Her scent taunted him—sweet, but not too sweet. And never forgotten, not even after seven years.

She said his name once more. "Mack."

Her hand closed on his arm, gently, with care. He covered her hand with his own. She pulled and he followed where she led, back to the balcony door. They stood looking out at the ocean and the night.

"When my mother died," she said, "the very hardest thing, the thing that seemed impossible to me, was that I would never have any more memories of her. What I had up till that point was it. There was no possibility that there would be more between us than there had already been. No more little moments ahead that would later come flashing back when I thought of her—no more things she might say that would stick in my mind, no more hugs, no more smiles. I'd had them. All the hugs and the smiles she would ever give me…"

Mack gave no response. He couldn't. What she had just said was so exactly what he'd felt, back in his mother's house, when he'd looked at that ceramic menagerie in the kitchen window and remembered his mother's soft voice in his ear, calling him Mackie, showing him her treasures, cautioning him of their fragility.

Jenna laid her head against his shoulder. Her corn-silk hair brushed his arm. It felt so warm, her hair. And it tickled a little.

He wanted to turn to her, pull her close and lower his mouth to hers. But he didn't. He knew damn well that right then it was comfort she offered and nothing more. He wanted it, the comfort. He would spoil it if he made a move on her.

"One thing I don't think I'll ever understand," he heard himself say.

"What?"

"How she could be married to a man for all those years and never tell him the truth."

He felt her hair whisper against his arm as she looked up at him. "You never told me the truth about her. You led me to believe that she'd died years ago."

He realized he'd forgotten to breathe. So he did. Very carefully, letting out the breath he hadn't known he'd been holding. "I wanted to tell you. You were the only one I ever wanted to tell."

"But you didn't."

"Because I also wanted to forget."

"And did it work? Did you forget?"

They both knew the answer, but he said it anyway. "No. Eventually, I had to deal with it, with her. Hell, I'm still dealing with it."

"You did a good job today—of dealing with it."

"Thanks." He still wanted to kiss her. He wanted it pretty badly. But he didn't try it.

Even for a man who didn't mind taking chances, there were some things too precious to risk—things like how far they'd come toward each other during the bleak day just passed.

She had her arm wrapped in his and her head on his shoulder.

For right then, it was plenty. It was more than enough.

Chapter 8

When Jenna retired to her own section of the suite, she called Lacey at home. She wanted to see how things were going at the store and to let her sister know where they were staying. She waited as the phone rang, her nerves a little on edge, thinking how far away Meadow Valley seemed right then, wondering what kind of questions Lacey would ask and how she could effectively explain all that had happened since Mack had picked her up that morning.

It turned out she didn't have to explain anything. Lacey wasn't there. Jenna left a brief message, just the address and phone number of the hotel.

The next morning Mack ordered breakfast for them in the suite. It was a little windy to enjoy the balcony, so they ate at the glass-topped table in the living area.

As Jenna spooned up poached eggs and nibbled her

toast, she couldn't help thinking of other breakfasts they'd shared.

The very first one, for instance, in his L.A. apartment. He'd gotten up before her and run down to the corner convenience store, bringing back two large coffees and half a dozen chocolate-frosted cake doughnuts with sprinkles on top.

He'd bent over her and kissed her awake. "I've brought breakfast. Breakfast in bed."

She'd sat up among the pillows and wrapped herself in the sheet. He'd passed her one of the coffees, his warm fingers brushing hers, a casual contact that thrilled her to her toes. No coffee before or since had ever tasted so good.

They hadn't been able to stop looking at each other, *grinning* at each other. Her hair was all tangled and her makeup had rubbed off and she felt like the most beautiful woman in the world. It was all very smug and magical and right.

She'd barely enjoyed one doughnut when he was reaching for her and pushing her down among the pillows. Later, when they got up to shower together, he found two little sugar sprinkles pressed into her back, right at the ridge of her shoulder blade. He licked them off.

Perhaps that had been the best breakfast of her life. And she'd shared it with Mack.

The worst one had been with Mack, too. In their New York apartment, about a week before Jenna decided on the visit home—the one from which she would never return.

It was an awful, silent breakfast for the most part.

She remembered the clink of their spoons stirring coffee, the way he so carefully spread jam on his toast.

He'd come in very late the night before, from one of those meetings that somehow always managed to go on till all hours. She'd been asleep, but she woke when she heard him enter the bedroom.

She had lain there turned away from him, trying to keep her breathing shallow and slow. It had come to that point with them, the point where she faked sleep when he came home late. Where she avoided his eyes at the table. Where she gave him her cheek to kiss instead of her lips, because she knew that if she looked right at him, all the things she wanted to tell him, all the things he kept refusing to hear, would come spilling out all over again—and to absolutely no avail.

Avoidance was the order of the day by then. So she lay there on her side, measuring her own breathing.

But after he'd taken off his clothes and climbed in beside her, the hopelessness of their life together had struck her like a sudden blow. The tears had come welling up.

He had heard her whimpering as she tried to stifle her sobs. "Damn it, Jenna. It's late. I'm beat. Don't start this now."

They'd ended up shouting at each other—or rather, he had shouted. She had wept and pleaded.

And then, the next morning at breakfast, there had been silence.

Until she had glanced across at him spreading jam on his toast so very carefully and her mouth had opened and there she was, begging him again.

"Mack, please. I just want a baby, Mack. If I only had a baby, I could—"

He stopped her with a look. Then he dropped his toast onto his plate, got up from the table and went out the door.

The worst breakfast of her life. Yes, it had definitely been that one in all its hideous hurtful silence, shared, as the best had been, with the man across the table from her now.

Mack picked up his coffee cup, drank and met her eyes over the rim. He was wearing a polo shirt and chinos, clothing she'd noted with some relief when she emerged from her own room to find him sitting in an easy chair reading the *Los Angeles Times.* She'd worried just a little that she might catch him in a robe, or without his shirt, or in some other distracting state of semiundress.

But no. He'd played it straight.

Mack set his coffee cup in its saucer. "Deep thoughts?"

She had the urge to speak frankly, to admit she'd been thinking about the rough times they'd had. And to say that she believed he'd been right in not wanting children back then. From a more mature perspective she realized that having a baby rarely saved a marriage—or effectively consoled a neglected wife. Now she could see how the demands of a little one would only have made their problems worse. And that when the inevitable breakup did come, an innocent child would have been stuck in the middle.

However, if she admitted that he'd been right to say no to a baby back then, she wouldn't be able to stop herself from asking him how he felt about having children now.

She wasn't sure she ought to do that just yet. The

issue had once been a heavily charged one. To bring it up now would only dredge up old hurts.

And it could also be a step toward real intimacy with him. Not long ago she would have sworn she would never take such a step.

Now she had to admit she felt differently. She'd reached the point where she couldn't swear to anything.

He was watching her. Waiting to hear whatever she might reveal.

"It's nothing," she lied.

She knew by the smile he gave her that he didn't believe her. But he didn't press her.

"More coffee?" He picked up the pot from the warmer.

"I'd love some." She held out her cup.

When they got to Alec's house, Lois had left for the supermarket.

"She's got a list a mile long," Alec said. "She's a dynamo. She's always been like that, the type who takes charge. Ordinarily, it irritates me. But right now, I'm grateful. I need someone taking charge."

Jenna glanced around the kitchen. It did indeed look as if Lois had been busy. The stack of unopened mail had vanished from the table and the air smelled more of cleaning products than of cigarettes. It appeared that the floor had been mopped. Also, the sink was free of dirty dishes.

"Coffee?" Alec offered. He gestured toward the coffeemaker. The pot was half full. "It's made."

Both Jenna and Mack declined.

"Well, then." Alec pointed toward the living room, down the short hall perpendicular to the front door.

"Go on in and sit down. I'll get you those things I mentioned."

Jenna and Mack filed into the living room, but neither of them felt like sitting. They stood side by side in the center of the room, between the television and the maple coffee table, which bore a basket arrangement of dried flowers and a neat fan of *National Geographic*s.

"Sit down, sit down." It was Alec, appearing from the hall that led to the back of the house. He was toting a big cardboard box and had a pair of half-lensed reading glasses perched on his nose. "Mack, would you shove those magazines out of the way?"

Mack didn't move. Jenna shot him a glance. He had a look in his eyes that she couldn't quite read. "Alec. Listen. We don't have to open it now. I'll just take it with me and—"

"Please." The older man's voice wasn't much more than a croak. He coughed. "There's so much I don't know, so much I wish I could understand. I would be so grateful, if you'd only let me..." He fell silent. Then he sighed. "I'm sorry. Of course I have no right to ask such a thing. This box is yours, not mine." He made a move to hand Mack the box.

Mack hesitated, but only for a fraction of a second. Then he turned, picked up the magazines and tossed them under the coffee table. "Put it down here, Alec."

Alec held on to the box. "Are you certain?"

"Yeah. Come on."

So Alec set the box on the table. Then he and Mack sat on opposite ends of the sofa. Jenna took a side chair.

The box was taped securely shut. Alec produced a utility knife, which he handed to Mack. Jenna realized her heart had started beating a little faster as Mack slit the tape and turned back the flaps.

Mack pulled out photo albums first. There were three of them. They were numbered, the numbers written by hand on cards tucked into plastic pockets on the spines. Mack opened the first one.

Jenna couldn't really see from her seat across the table. She stood and craned forward. Mack saw her problem and slid toward the center of the sofa, leaving a space for her on his right. She took the seat he offered. He gave her a smile. Without even thinking about it, she moved a little closer to him.

They spent an hour just turning pages. Mack was able to pick out Bridget and Claire. And his own very young self. He recognized his parents, too. His mother, tiny and pretty, stood in front of a slightly run-down California bungalow-style house, holding on to his father's arm and smiling bravely into the sun.

Once they had looked through all the albums, they found school progress reports, three of them for Bridget and one for Mack. Instead of A's and B's, Mack's report showed S's and O's, for "Satisfactory" and "Outstanding." N.I. meant "Needs Improvement." He had only one of those, in the category of "Follows Instructions."

Beyond the albums and the report cards, they discovered a number of drawings made by very young hands. There were also little swatches of baby hair and three tiny first teeth wrapped in squares of white silk. They found three sets of knit booties, one blue and two pink. And birth announcements, birthday party invitations, other small articles of clothing: tiny knit hats and a yellow bib. There were rattles and two small dolls, a tattered brown teddy bear and a dog-eared Little Golden Book of a Christmas story titled *Noel*.

"All those years we were together…" Alec shook his head. "She never said a word. But she had what we used to call her sad times, when she would hardly smile, when she'd have a certain miles-away look in her eyes. At first I would ask her what was wrong. But she would only pat my cheek, tell me, 'It's one of my sad times, Al, that's all….'"

Alec readjusted his glasses on the end of his nose. "After our first few years together, I just accepted that the sad times were a part of who she was. I knew they would come, and that eventually they would pass. But I never knew why. Not until a few hours before she died. I…" Alec seemed to catch himself. He looked from Mack to Jenna. "Maybe you'd rather not hear all this."

Jenna waited for Mack to answer, but the silence stretched out too long. She couldn't bear it. "No," she said, "Really. Please…"

To her relief, Mack spoke up then. "Yeah. It's okay. Go ahead."

"All right. I… Well, isn't that strange? I can't remember exactly what I was—"

Jenna suggested softly, "You said you never understood your wife's sad times, until a few hours before she died."

"Oh. Yes, of course. That's right. All those years. I never knew the cause of them. And then, the day she died, I was sitting by her bed, holding her hand and…she told me." He looked at Mack. "About you. About the girls. She said she knew almost nothing about Bridget and Claire. That she hadn't seen them, hadn't heard from them, or about them, in all the years since she'd given them up. But that you had come looking for her. That you had grown into a fine man. You were wealthy and successful, a lawyer. She spoke of you with such pride. She said you had told her that her daughters were doing all right. She asked me to call you, said she needed to see you. She explained about this box then. She said that whatever happened, I had to make sure you got it. I promised her I'd take care of it."

Alec picked up a folded square of yellowed construction paper. Carefully he unfolded it to reveal a stick-figure family beneath a big yellow sun. In the lower right-hand corner, the name Bridget was written in red crayon.

One by one Alec touched the smiling stick-figure faces: father, mother, daughters, son. "She was telling me this impossible, incredible thing. That she'd had a whole family I never knew about. I should have had a thousand questions. I *do* have a thousand questions. Now. But then…nothing. Then, I was just plain scared. I only wanted to give her whatever she needed, make any promises she had to hear. I knew the worst was coming, that I was losing her.

"And *she* knew, too, didn't she?" Alec looked to Mack for an answer, but Mack said nothing. So the older man looked beyond Mack, at Jenna. "Don't you think she must have known that she didn't have long?"

Jenna had no answer, either. She gave what she could, a sad look and a shrug.

Alec refolded the stick-figure family and gently set them next to the stack of albums. Then, with great care, he took a swatch of silk in his hand. He peeled it open and stared at the tiny tooth inside. "I told her from the first that I didn't want children. I told her I was set in my ways. That I wanted us to have our freedom, I wanted her all to myself."

He swallowed, shook his head. "Later, after a few years, I started to see things differently. I told her that maybe it would be nice…a little boy, or a little girl."

He slid a finger and thumb up under the dark frames of his glasses and rubbed at his eyes. "But she never got pregnant. Now I'll always wonder…was it on purpose? Because I had said once that I didn't want children? Or because she couldn't forgive herself, couldn't let herself have another baby after the ones she'd given up? It's so sad. She didn't understand how much I loved her, how much I could have accepted the longer and longer I loved her. How I would have wanted to go looking to find you. If she'd only told me. If I'd only known…"

It was after two when Jenna and Mack stowed the box of keepsakes in the trunk of the Lincoln and headed for the hotel. Mack had been ready to leave much earlier, but Lois had returned and insisted that he and Jenna stay for lunch. So they'd all sat around the kitchen table for a while as Lois bustled about getting the food ready. Then they ate. After the meal, there were cookies and coffee.

Lois kept the conversation going. She chattered away about how things had changed in Long Beach since her last visit and how much she enjoyed her life in Arizona. Jenna asked questions and made interested noises. The men were mostly silent.

Mack didn't have much to say during the drive to the hotel, either, which was all right with Jenna. Looking through Doreen's secret box of keepsakes had been difficult even for her—and she wasn't the husband from whom Doreen's secret had been kept, or the son Doreen had given away.

When they got to the suite, Jenna checked the hotel phone. The message light was dark: no calls. Mack pulled out his cell phone and punched up a number.

Jenna dropped her shoulder bag on a side table and wandered over to the chair where Mack had laid his newspaper earlier that morning. She sat down and began glancing through it, tuning out Mack's phone conversation.

But then she heard him say, "Yes. To Miami, the next flight you can find me."

Jenna set down the paper and listened, bewildered and beginning to get angry, as he made reservations for two to Florida.

By the time he hung up, she was on her feet. He started to punch up another number, but got only half-way through it before she commanded, "Wait a minute, Mack."

He punched the off button and looked at her impatiently. "What?"

"What are you doing?"

He made one of those noises that always used to drive her crazy in the old days—a low, intolerant, utterly contemptuous sound. "What does it look like?"

"It looks like you're making arrangements to leave."

"Very perceptive."

Her irritation was increasing. "I don't like this, Mack. It feels way too much like old times."

Now he was glaring at her.

Thank God she was a thirty-year-old woman now, much too mature to be intimidated by a man's facial expression. "Yes," she said, "just like old times. You've got the phone in your hand. You're making reservations. You think you're flying to Florida right away and you also think that I'm going with you. Is that correct?"

He made a growling sound that she decided to consider an answer in the affirmative.

She continued, "You think we're flying to Florida. And have you discussed this with me at all? Have you asked me what I think about it, if I want to go, if I'm even *willing* to go? No. You have not. As I said, it's just like old times, when you thought nothing of taking a job in New York City and then informing me that we were moving." She gave him her sourest smile. "You know, Mack, if I didn't mind being kept in the dark about major decisions, I might have stayed married to you."

"You *are* married to me."

"You keep saying that."

"Because it's true."

"When you behave in this manner, it only reminds me that if I can just get through the next twelve days, you'll never be able to say that again."

He tossed the phone on a low table a few feet away from him. Jenna winced when it hit. "It's my damn week, remember? It's supposed to be my choice where we go."

That gave her pause. He did have a point. She'd hardly consulted him when she'd chosen Wyoming for *her* week.

And now, looking more closely at him, into those gray-blue eyes, she could see the pain he imagined he could outrun.

"I'm finished here, Jenna. I've got that damn box my mother left me and I'm sorry I didn't get here in time to hear whatever she had to say to me. We spent yesterday doing what we could for Alec. Now his sister is here. He'll manage all right. I've got five days left in my week. And I want to spend them *my* way. I want to show you my house, take you out on my boat. I want what I asked for in the first place. Time together, just you and me."

At that moment, she actually wished she could give him what he said he wanted. But she knew it wouldn't be right. "Well, I'm sorry." She put real effort into making her voice gentler than before. "We have to stay for the funeral."

"My mother is dead, Jenna. She's not going to care if I miss her funeral."

"Oh, Mack. Haven't you heard? Funerals aren't for the dead. They're for the rest of us. And your stepfather needs you to be there for this one."

"Damn it, I only met the man yesterday. I can call him right now and tell him we've got to leave. It's not going to kill him if I don't stick it out to the end."

"Maybe it's not. But it will hurt him, and he has been hurt enough. And Mack, I think it would mean so much to him, I honestly do, to have you there at her funeral. It would show him that you're able to do what has to be done, that you turned out all right. You turned out to be the kind of man who knows how to forgive."

"Hell. I forgive her. I think Alec knows that."

"Then you'll reinforce that knowledge. Because that man really likes you, Mack, that man wants a connection with you. In a way, if you think about it, you're the closest he'll ever come to having a child."

His lips made a flat line. "It's too late for that. I'm nobody's child."

"Of course you're not. But you know what I'm getting at. You know what you have to do. I'm sorry that it hurts you. But there's no getting away from it. You talk about how you've forgiven your mother. Do you think you'll be able to forgive yourself if we run off to Florida right now?"

He didn't answer immediately, but when he did, her heart rose. "All right, damn it. We'll stay."

They stood near the glass door to the balcony. Beyond the glass, it was a gorgeous Southern California day. The sky was the softest, palest of blues, dotted here and there with white cotton-puff clouds. Gulls wheeled above the golden stretch of beach below them and a few young mothers with toddlers sat beneath bright umbrellas in the sand. The sea looked calm as glass.

Jenna wanted to touch the man beside her, so she went ahead and did it. She took his arm, the way she had the night before, and, as she had then, she rested her head on his shoulder. "This is a lovely hotel. And look at that beach. Key West might be fabulous, but this isn't half-bad. Long Beach has become a real resort area. See those islands out there, with all those cute small hotels on them?"

He chuckled. "Jenna. Those are dressed-up oil derricks."

"You are kidding me."

"Nope. They've been there for years. The Disney people came up with the look. They put a false front on them and light them at night. Very attractive."

"You could have fooled me."

"I think I heard somewhere that they're named after dead astronauts. Island Chaffee, Island Grissom. The oil industry here is nothing if not innovative."

A thought came to her—a way to make their stay a little more bearable to him. She lifted her head and their eyes met. "I'll tell you what, since you're being so gracious about this—"

He pretended to scoff. "Gracious? Now, there's a word I'll bet you never thought you'd use in conjunction with me."

She laughed. It felt good, standing there at his side, overlooking the Pacific, her arm in his and a feeling of real accomplishment spreading through her.

In the old days, at this point, she would have been crying and Mack would have been packing their suitcases to go.

But this wasn't the old days. She was stronger than she had been then. And he was...gentler, more willing to let her have her say.

"That's right," she said. "*Gracious* was never a word I would have used to describe you. But I'm using it now. And since you *are* being gracious, I can be gracious, too."

The grin he gave her sent a shiver racing along the surface of her skin. "Does this mean you're giving up on those damn separate rooms?"

She clucked her tongue. "Dream on."

"Excuse me. I don't consider making love with you a dream. I consider it a very real possibility."

"Consider it whatever you want. I said separate rooms and I meant what I said."

He had stopped grinning. The look in his eyes melted her midsection and did that embarrassing wobbly thing to her knees.

He turned, so quickly that it startled her. She might have backed up, but he gave her no chance. He reached for her and hauled her close. With a sharp gasp of surprise, she splayed her hands against his chest.

"Mack." It was a warning, one he didn't heed.

Before she could order him to let go, his mouth came down and covered hers.

Chapter 9

Apparently, some things never changed.

It was that moment at the door to Mack's L.A. apartment all over again, even all these years later.

Jenna heard her own small cry as Mack's mouth opened over hers. She stopped pushing him away and slid her hands upward, over his big, solid shoulders. His tongue found hers and danced with it.

She couldn't help herself. She stroked the back of his neck. She had always loved that, the feel of his skin at the nape, the texture of the hair that his barber cut with electric clippers, silky and stubbly at the same time. She pulled him closer. And he did the same to her, nestling her hips along his thighs, so that she could feel his desire for her, there against her lower belly.

Oh, she was melting. Yes, all softness. All willingness.

Though she shouldn't.

Shouldn't do this.

Shouldn't give in to this.

This wonder…

This glory…

His hands roamed her back, sliding over her hips one minute, cupping her the next and pulling her even closer—and then moving upward, so that he could tangle his fingers in the strands of her hair.

His tongue went on playing with hers.

And she played back.

Oh, how lovely. Playing back. She and Mack played so well together. They had from the first.

And oh, how easy it would be to fall right into playing again…

How delicious and lovely…

But she couldn't.

She really couldn't.

With a sigh that was part regret and part determination, she put her hands flat against his chest again and broke the kiss. "No, Mack."

He opened his eyes and stared down at her. He didn't look happy. She moved in his arms, signaling clearly that she wanted him to let her go.

He did, but he also asked, "Why not?"

She longed to fling out a quick and flippant response. But they both deserved better. They deserved—and they needed—as much honesty as they could bear, wherever this two weeks together ended up taking them.

She said, "Because making love was always so good with us. Sometimes I think it was too good. Sometimes I wonder if it was all we had, really. A great sex life, as you said the other day."

He was shaking his head. "No. There was more. You know there was."

"Do I? You were on your way to make it big at any cost. And I was getting a business degree, getting a little taste of the larger world before I went home and opened my store and married Logan and raised a family. We...intersected over Byron. And there was this attraction. Maybe it was only physical, did you ever think about that? Maybe all that was good was the sex and that's why it didn't last."

"Jenna." He made her name into a tender rebuke. "How can you say it didn't last? We're both here now, aren't we?"

She held her ground on that one. "It *was* ended. We agreed on the terms of a divorce."

"But we didn't go through with it."

"*I* went through with it. You were the one who didn't sign the papers."

"And you never came looking for me to find out where they were."

"I did come looking for you. I came looking for you two weeks ago. I asked you—"

"Wait a minute."

She folded her arms across her middle and let out a small sound of irritation. "What?"

"Do we really need to go into all this again?"

She caught her lower lip between her teeth, worried it a little, then let it go. "No. You're right. We don't. All I'm trying to say is that I'm not allowing the sexual part of our relationship to take over everything again. I want a little balance. I want to be sure we've got more in common than how good it feels making love together."

"So. You're admitting we do have *something,* then?"

"Yes. I am. And as I was trying to tell you before you distracted me, I'm willing to give a little ground here."

He looked doubtful. "You're kidding me. You? Giving ground?"

"Yes. Since you've been so gracious about staying for your mother's funeral, once the funeral's over, we can go to Key West—and stay until the two weeks are up."

A smile lit his eyes. He teased, "What about Wyoming and all those Bravos you want to get to know?"

"I guess Wyoming and my Bravo cousins will just have to wait. I'll get there. Someday." She looked out past the balcony again. "And I am thinking it might be nice to take a walk on the beach."

"Right now?"

"You have something better to do?"

"I did. But you turned me down."

"So?"

"So, let's go."

The red light on the hotel phone was blinking when they returned to the room an hour later. A message from Alec. Mack called him back.

Alec invited them to his house for dinner that night.

Mack wanted to decline. They'd spent last night taking care of Alec. Tonight, he'd imagined a long, intimate evening, just him and Jenna.

But before he could make their excuses, Jenna spoke up. "It's Alec? What's up?"

And he had to ask Alec to hold on while he told her about the invitation. And naturally, she thought they should go.

And hell. So did he.

He told Alec they'd be there.

He hung up and turned to Jenna. She was standing a few feet away in front of the gilt-framed mirror near the door, brushing out the tangles the wind had put in her hair. He went to her, stopping just behind her. Their eyes met in the mirror.

"Six-thirty," he said. "For cocktails. For dinner, Lois is whipping up something called chicken fiesta."

"Sounds interesting." She touched the tip of the brush to her pretty, slightly pointed chin. "But somehow, I didn't picture Alec as the type to serve cocktails—and on Tuesday night, too."

"Maybe it's just to impress us."

He'd meant the remark jokingly, but she actually considered it. "Maybe. But my bet is that he wants to make you feel at home. Your mother told him you were wealthy and successful. He probably thinks you drink cocktails every night. Isn't that what all millionaires do?"

He shrugged. His mind wasn't really on Alec. He could smell the salt air on her skin. Her cheeks shone pink from the wind and the sun. She looked so clean and fresh and…wholesome.

Yes. That was the word for Jenna: *wholesome.* He'd never imagined until he'd first set eyes on her how utterly erotic wholesomeness could be. She parted that silky yellow hair of hers in the middle and it fell straight to her shoulders in a simple, classic style.

With a finger, very slowly, he lifted a section of that shining hair away from the side of her neck.

Hazel eyes darkened. "Mack…"

"Shh."

He lowered his head and put his lips against her

neck, tasted the sweetness of her skin and the tang the sea wind had left there. She allowed the caress, even surrendered so much as to let out a soft sigh.

But he played fair. He didn't linger. He would keep their agreement on the issue of lovemaking.

For the moment, anyway.

He met her eyes in the mirror again. "So. We've got what? Maybe an hour to kill?"

"I've got sand in my shoes. I was just thinking I'd take a shower and change my clothes."

"I'd offer to wash your back for you, but unfortunately..."

"I'd have to say no."

"You wouldn't *have* to say no."

"Oh, yes, I would."

She left him, disappearing into her private section of the suite. He called and changed the plane reservations from tomorrow to late Saturday morning. Then he prowled the main room for a while, trying not to picture Jenna in the shower, the water cascading over her, running between her full breasts, tracing glittery rivulets along her smooth belly and slithering down into the golden curls between her slim legs.

Finally he went to his own room and took a shower of his own—a quick, cold one.

Alec had made a giant pitcher of margaritas. They sat on the back patio around a glass-topped table in chairs with floral-patterned cushions.

"Dory always loved it back here," Alec said.

Jenna could understand why. The yard was cozy and well cared for, with a green stretch of lawn and bougainvillea spilling over the tall redwood fence.

Alec talked about his employment agency, Telford Temporaries, where he and Doreen had met. He'd sold the business just last year. He and Doreen had planned to do some serious traveling.

"We took a cruise last winter." His eyes had a faraway look. "The Mediterranean. From Lisbon to Barcelona in ten days. We strolled the Casbah in Tangier, went to the Central Market in Casablanca, visited that medieval cathedral in Palma de Mallorca and…" He seemed to shake himself. "Well. Let me just say, we had a wonderful time."

He asked about Mack's life. "Dory mentioned you live in Florida. Are you with some big law firm there?"

Mack said that he didn't practice law anymore and explained how he was able to live on his investments.

Lois spoke up then. "So Jenna, do you live in Florida, too?"

"No. I live up north. Meadow Valley. It's a little town in the—"

"Oh, yes. In the foothills. One of the gold rush towns, right? I hear it's lovely there."

"I like it."

"My brother tells me that you and Mack are… friends?"

Jenna began to feel a bit uncomfortable at that point. "Yes. That's right."

Her discomfort increased when Lois asked, "So then, how did you two meet?"

Jenna cast a quick glance Mack's way. No help there. He was sipping his margarita with one eyebrow annoyingly raised. She knew just what he was thinking: go ahead. Tell her.

And why shouldn't she? There was nothing to be ashamed of.

Jenna sipped from her own drink, gathering a little false courage and her thoughts, as well. Finally she said, "Mack and I were married once. We divorced, but it turned out the divorce was never finalized. So now we're…"

"Trying again," Lois provided, her tanned face lighting up and the wrinkles around her eyes deepening as she grinned.

No, not exactly, Jenna almost said. But then she reconsidered. "Trying again" didn't sound bad at all. Why muddy things up with confusing details neither Alec nor Lois needed to know?

Lois had turned to her brother, who sat to her left. "See? Didn't I tell you that they had to be much more than just friends?"

Alec nodded. "You did, Lois. That's exactly what you said."

Jenna sipped more of her margarita and resisted the urge to glance at Mack. She knew what she would see if she looked at him, anyway: humor in his eyes and a big grin on his sexy mouth. She didn't need that.

"A refill?" Alec asked.

Well, what do you know? Her glass was empty. And such nice big glasses they were, too. "Yes, please. These margaritas are excellent."

By the time Lois served the chicken, Jenna was starting to feel just a bit tipsy. When Alec offered another refill, she politely turned it down.

She wished she'd never had that second one, because during the meal Alec said something about the possibility of Mack approaching his sisters with the news that their mother had died.

Mack managed to avoid giving the older man an answer. He did it quite skillfully, saying he'd think about it, but that right now they should just concentrate on getting through the funeral.

Alec, the dear old sweetheart, backed right off. And Lois patted his hand and told him Mack was probably right.

The whole exchange was over before Jenna, in her pleasant margarita haze, could put her two cents in. She would have brought the subject up again, but the moment never seemed quite right. And besides, dangerous subjects were always best raised when a woman had her wits fully about her—especially dangerous subjects that concerned Mack McGarrity.

They left for the hotel at a little after ten. The big car had a very smooth and quiet ride. Jenna couldn't resist leaning back and closing her eyes.

She woke to the feel of Mack's lips brushing her ear. "You planning to sleep in the car tonight?"

It seemed so natural, to make a sleepy sound, to turn her mouth to his and—

She stopped herself just in time. "Let's go in."

His lips were only an inch from hers. And his eyes looked dark and full of sensual secrets that he just might be willing to share with her.

His mouth brushed hers, once, then he whispered, "Did we ever make love in a car? I don't remember it. I doubt that it's something I would have forgotten."

They hadn't, but she didn't tell him that. He would probably only take it as an invitation to try it now.

All she said was "Mack," and she shook her head.

He mimicked her movement, his head going back and forth in time with her own.

Then he turned to his door and leaned on the handle.

The next day, over breakfast, Jenna told Mack that he really ought to consider getting in touch with his sisters.

He said, "I think that's my decision to make."

"But—"

"Let it go, Jenna. It's not for you to decide."

Though she pressed her lips together in obvious disapproval, she did let the subject drop.

Then, after breakfast, she suggested that she and Mack should take Alec and Lois out that night.

Mack tried to demur. It was about time they had a damn evening alone, he thought.

But Jenna wouldn't let it go. "Call him. He had us over to his house last night, and I'm sure it'll be good for him to get out for a while."

"Did it ever occur to you that maybe he's not in the mood to get out?"

She picked up the phone and shoved it in his direction. "Ask him. Let him answer for himself. And let him choose the restaurant. Someplace he feels comfortable."

Mack let her stand there for a count of five, holding out the phone and glaring at him. As he made her wait, he indulged in a moment of nostalgia, recalling how sweet and malleable she'd been when she was younger.

Then, with a heavy sigh, he gave in and made the damn call. Alec said that he and his sister would love to go out to dinner with them.

"Now what?" Mack asked, after he'd called the restaurant Alec had chosen and learned that reservations would not be required. "I suppose you have something really constructive planned for today."

She pinched up her mouth at him. "You have some problem with constructive activities?"

"Hell, no. But I'd rather take it easy, enjoy ourselves, just you and me."

"Well, actually, I was thinking…"

"Stand back."

"Very funny. Remember that day we drove down to Seal Beach?"

He did. "It was a Sunday, I think. In June. We had a day off and no money and we got in the car and headed south. We had our swimsuits with us. We changed on a side street, right in that old Chrysler I had. Remember? You made me stand guard while you were changing, though you never did explain to me what the hell I was supposed to do if someone dared to peek in."

She laughed. "Lord. I remember that."

It had been a good day, one of the last of the good days, as a matter of fact. Not long after, Mack had taken the job in New York.

Mack said, "Seal Beach is damn easy to get to from here."

"That's just what I was thinking."

The drive took less than half an hour. They found parking on a side street, then strolled down tree-shaded, brick-lined Main, wandering in and out of any shops that caught their eye. Jenna picked up a few souvenirs, among them a melon-colored T-shirt for Lacey and a fur-covered toy mouse for Byron. When they tired of shopping, they sat for a while in grassy Eisenhower

Park, then chose one of the restaurants near the pier for lunch.

They even wandered over to Surfside Beach to watch the surfers floating on their bright-colored boards, waiting for the perfect wave—which, at least during the half hour that Jenna and Mack observed them, never seemed to come along.

When they returned to the hotel to get ready for dinner, Jenna detoured straight to the phone. No message light.

Mack had carried in the bags of souvenirs. He dropped them onto a chair. "You're expecting an important call?"

"No. I'm just beginning to worry a little about Lacey. I called her and left the number here on Monday. I thought that she'd at least check in, let me know she got the message."

"You think she might be up to her old tricks?"

She sent him a look. "What old tricks?"

"The way I remember it, during the time you and I were married, she ran away from home about a half dozen times."

Jenna jumped to her sister's defense. "She was a teenager then. And she had problems."

"That doesn't answer my question."

"All right. No, I do not think she's run away from home. She's very responsible now. She keeps her agreements. And besides, what good would it do her to run away from Meadow Valley? She doesn't even live there anymore."

Mack muttered something about feminine logic, then added, "If you're worried about her, call her again."

She picked up the phone, dialed—and got her own

voice on the answering machine. This time she left a message asking Lacey to please call the hotel right away. She hung up, picturing Byron wandering the rooms of her mother's house, starved for both Fancy Feast and companionship.

She dialed Linen and Lace. Marla, her head clerk, said that yes, Lacey had been in both yesterday and the day before to take care of the receipts. Jenna hung up from that call feeling moderately relieved.

Then Mack said, "We've got to pick up Alec and Lois at seven. If you want one of those half-hour showers of yours, you'd better get moving."

"I do not take half-hour showers."

He smiled. Very slowly. "How much do you want to bet?"

"Oh. Right. And then you'd have to time me, wouldn't you? I don't think so."

"You have a suspicious mind."

"Only where you're concerned."

They stared each other down for a minute, then he commanded gruffly, "Take your damn shower."

He looked so…huggable right then, those gold eyebrows scrunched together and the corners of his mouth drawn low. If she hadn't been exercising such care to avoid physical contact with him, she would have kissed him hard and possessively, right on the mouth.

Lacey did call, just as Mack and Jenna were leaving for Alec's house.

"Hi." Lacey laughed, a breathless sound. "Listen, I promise you, the cat is fine and the store is fine. And I know I should have gotten back to you sooner, but every time I thought of it, it was either midnight or four in the morning or some other totally inappropriate time."

Jenna thought Lacey sounded nervous, even a little bit manic. "Lace, are you okay?"

"Of course. So what's going on? I thought you were supposed to be riding the range in Wyoming this week."

Mack was standing by the door. He lifted an eyebrow at her. Jenna gave him a nod, mouthed, "Just a minute."

Then she spoke to her sister again. "Mack's mother died. We're here in Southern California until the funeral on Friday. Then we'll go to Mack's house in Key West. We're skipping Wyoming, after all. But I'll call you from Florida as soon as we get there."

"Wait a minute. I thought you told me that Mack McGarrity was an orphan."

Jenna glanced at Mack again. He was leaning against the door—waiting with reasonable patience, actually. "It's a long story. I'll explain it all when I get home."

"Is it…going well, between you two?"

Jenna smiled. "You know, all in all, I do believe it is."

"Well. Good." Now, what was she hearing in Lacey's voice? Relief? Satisfaction?

Unfortunately, she had no time right then to ask. "Listen, we're just going out the door, taking Mack's stepfather out to dinner."

Lacey showed no inclination to linger, either. "Okay. Have fun. Call me from Florida."

"I will."

They went to a restaurant Alec liked in Huntington Beach, where the menu offered a dozen varieties of fresh fish each day. Alec seemed very quiet through the meal. He admitted on the way home that maybe he hadn't been ready yet to go back to one of the places he used to visit with Doreen.

Mack glanced significantly at Jenna. She read his look. *I told you he wasn't ready for a night on the town.*

When they got to the house, Alec asked if they'd like to come in for coffee. Jenna would have said yes, but Mack clamped a hand over her arm. A shiver of excitement sizzled through her, distracting her enough that she didn't object when Mack said, "Thanks Alec. But I think we'll just go on back to the hotel."

In the suite, Mack found two miniature brandy bottles in the well-stocked bar. He poured one for each of them. Then, brandy in hand, he sat on one of the sofas and put his feet up on a hassock. Jenna wandered to the glass door that led to the balcony and looked out on the harbor lights. She sipped, and couldn't help smiling to herself as she thought that those lovely little island hotels were actually oil derricks.

Then Alec came to mind and she felt her smile fade away.

"Why the frown?"

She turned. Mack was watching her.

He patted the space beside him on the sofa. She started to move toward him, then reconsidered. They probably shouldn't be getting too cozy. She shook her head and murmured ruefully, "Better not."

Mack's jaw tightened. He glanced past her, his fine mouth a hard line. She knew what he was doing: calling himself away from the brink of saying something he might regret. Finally he laid his arm along the sofa back and looked right at her again.

She decided to go on as if the uncomfortable moment hadn't occurred. "I was just…thinking of Alec. How hard it must be for him. They had a lot of years together, he and your mother. And it seems that they were happy years, for the most part."

Mack said nothing.

She could feel his irritation with her and she tried again to brush it off, this time with an offhand shrug. Still, he said nothing. She turned to look out over the harbor again.

That was when he deigned to speak. "Do you want me to agree with you, that Alec has it rough right now?"

She looked at him once more. "You don't have to agree with me, Mack. It's a fact."

"Yes, it is. A fact. And I think we've done about all we can personally do about it."

"I wasn't implying that we should do anything more."

"Oh, come on." He knocked back a gulp of brandy and winced as it went down. "Give yourself a minute or two. You'll come up with five or six ways that we can help to ease the poor man's pain—ways that will give us more very good reasons not to be alone together." He studied her face for several seconds before adding, "You have so many creative methods of avoiding me."

She wanted to argue, but she couldn't. She *was* avoiding him—avoiding getting too close to him, either physically or emotionally. And why shouldn't she? She had carefully specified separate rooms when they'd set up this little two-week adventure. He'd agreed to her terms. There was no reason she should feel defensive about sticking to them.

But she did feel defensive. "You're irritated because I didn't sit beside you just now? Is that it?"

"Partly. You're constantly putting physical space between us. And you don't limit yourself to space. You put Alec between us. And my sisters, too."

"How?" she demanded, feeling suddenly self-righteous. Physical space, certainly. Alec, maybe. But his sisters? No way.

"If you could only get me to agree to it, we'd be spending the second half of our two weeks enjoying a little family reunion with Bridget and Claire." He swirled his brandy around in his glass, then sipped again. "Go ahead. Tell me that isn't true."

She couldn't. Because it was. She cleared her throat. "Well, Mack, I do think that you should—"

"Jenna. I know what you think. You've made it painfully clear. Will you give it a rest now?"

"But I just—"

He set his glass on the table, and not gently. "Damn it, Jenna. I am not going to hunt down my sisters. Look what happened when I found my mother. She asked me not to tell her husband that I existed. And then she died."

"Oh, please. As if she died just to spite you."

"That's not what I meant. My point is, she's gone. I found her only to lose her again. This time, for good— and I can see in those eyes of yours what you're thinking. Yes, she did tell Alec about me in the end. And I'm here, sticking it out right through her funeral because you insisted. But after this, I'm finished. I've had enough of family reunions to last me a lifetime." He picked up his brandy again and drank the last of it. Then he set down the empty glass once more.

"And as for Alec," he said, "the man lost his wife. It hurts. And you personally are not going to be able to make it stop hurting. Only time will do that. If he's lucky." He stood. "I'm going to bed."

She let him get halfway across the room before she stopped him. "Mack."

He turned. "What?"

She admitted, "You're right. About Alec, anyway."

He didn't smile, but at least his expression relaxed a little. "I know I am. Good night." He went into his bedroom.

She whispered, "Good night, Mack," after he had shut the door.

The next day they drove up into the greater Los Angeles area. They visited Westwood Village, even drove by the apartment where they had met and been so happy together.

"It looks a little run-down."

"Mack. It looked a little run-down when we lived there."

"I guess. Maybe I just remember it through a kind of rosy haze."

His words pleased her, inordinately so. "You do?"

"It *was* a good time, Jenna."

"Yes. It was."

That little Italian place where they'd eaten that first night was still there. They couldn't resist going inside, where the light was dim and dusty plastic grapes hung from fake trellises overhead and between each of the booths.

They decided to go all out and order the meal they'd

shared that first night: salads and linguini with white clam sauce and a glass each of the house Chianti.

When the linguini came, Mack tasted it and shook his head. "It's not as good as I remember it."

She answered lightly, "Nothing ever is."

He looked at her across the table, his gaze tender and seeking as a caress. "I disagree. Some things are every bit as good. In fact, they're even better—or they could be, if you'd give them a chance."

"I think I am. Giving them a chance."

He grudgingly admitted that yes, she was. But he wished that she'd give them even more of a chance.

She twirled her fork in her linguini and decided it would be wiser not to reply.

After lunch they cruised east along Sunset, checking out the latest Rock and Roll billboards. And then they drove down Hollywood Boulevard, which was still just as tacky as both of them remembered.

It was after three when they headed back to Long Beach. Traffic was terrible. It took them an hour and a half to get to the hotel. They listened to an oldies station and sang along, inventing their own lyrics when the real words escaped them.

Mack caught her looking for a message light when they entered the suite.

"Uh-oh," he said. "No messages. No one calling us. No one we have to call. It's just you and me tonight."

She thought of dear, sweet Alec, and hoped he was all right. And she remembered her sister, that strange breathless quality to her voice. But she didn't mention either Doreen's husband or Lacey. It didn't seem the time for that, somehow.

Tomorrow there would be Doreen's funeral to get

through. They would call early to ask Alec if there was anything he needed, anything he'd like them to do.

But today was just for her and Mack. And the time had come when she had to admit to herself that she wanted it that way.

"A swim?" Mack said.

It sounded like a wonderful idea to her.

The temperature was in the low eighties. More than warm enough to sunbathe on deck chairs after a dip in the Olympic-size pool. They put two banana-style lounges head to head, lay down on their stomachs and whispered to each other as the water dried on their skin. After a while, Mack laid his cheek on his crossed arms and closed his eyes.

Jenna rested her chin on her hands and thought how really good he looked, so tanned and fit. She tried not to let her gaze linger on his strong arms, with their dusting of golden hair. She had always loved the feel of that hair. She used to put her hand on his arm, very lightly, not even really touching the skin, to feel that wonderful feathery silkiness against her palm.

She stared at the top of his golden head, at his strong shoulders and powerful back. The longing inside her was so strong right then—to reach out a hand, to touch. To say yes when he looked up with a certain question in his eyes.

Every day, every hour, every moment they spent together, Jenna found it a little more difficult to resist the pull between them.

He lifted his head. Her heart caught.

But then he only laid his other cheek against his arm without ever actually looking up. She heard him sigh.

And something inside her shifted.

Or maybe something fell away—an obstacle, an obstruction. An old, deep pain giving up, letting go, stepping aside so she could see the truth.

She was glad that he had come to find her. And glad that they were sharing this time together.

Did she still love him?

Oh, Lord. Probably. Most likely, she had never stopped.

But at this point, it didn't really matter what kind of label she put on it. If she called it love, or just desire, or the longing to try again.

What mattered was that up till now, she'd invested a lot of effort into keeping certain barriers between them.

From now on, that would change.

From now on, she intended to put heart, body and soul into tearing the barriers down.

Chapter 10

Mack could feel her watching him. He lifted his head.

One look into those shining hazel eyes and he knew.

So much for the damn separate rooms.

She gave him a quivery smile. "Let's go in the water again."

He couldn't right then. Everyone would have known exactly what was on his mind. "You go ahead."

"Sure?"

He nodded. He watched her walk toward the pool's edge, thinking she still looked every bit as good to him in the flesh as she'd looked in his dreams. She was slim and tall and she carried herself with a kind of quiet dignity he'd always admired. She wore a simple two-piece white suit that didn't reveal any more than it should. Wholesome. Yes. And achingly sexy at the same time.

But it wasn't only the way she looked. It was something else. Something indefinable. Some sweetness he'd never encountered before or since. Some...openness to him.

There had been other women. In the years without her.

Some had been kind and warm and funny, like Jenna. Some hadn't. None had lasted very long. After a while they had only reminded him of how much he missed what he'd once had with her.

She dived from the pool's edge, very neatly, cleaving the water with hardly a splash. Her crawl was as tidy as her dive, across the width of the pool and then back. She stopped near the edge, treading water, to trade a few words with a matronly woman in a flowered swim cap.

By then, Mack had his arousal under control enough to push himself off the banana lounge and onto his feet.

She looked his way and waved.

He went to join her in the water.

They got back to the room at a little after seven, both still wet from a final dip in the pool. They had closed the curtains earlier against the afternoon glare, so the main room of the suite was shadowed and cool. Maybe too cool. Jenna had her towel wrapped around her shoulders. She gathered it tighter.

"Why do they always think they have to keep it subzero in hotel rooms?" she asked through chattering teeth.

"There is a way to deal with that."

Her eyes widened. He knew what she thought he had meant.

And maybe he had. But just to be contrary, he turned and fiddled with the thermostat. "It should warm up in a minute or two." He turned back to find that she had closed the small distance between them.

She was still shivering. He did the natural thing and pulled her close. It felt good. Right, as it always had. Her hair was wet silk against his cheek. She smelled of chlorine, a smell about as far from erotic as any smell could get—or at least, he'd always thought so until now.

"Brr." She scrunched her shoulders, trying to get closer. He wrapped his arms a little tighter around her, enjoying the softness of her slim body beneath the towel, and waited for her shivers to subside.

He felt no need to try to tempt her anymore. No impulse to seduce.

Seduction, if there had actually been one, had already occurred. It had happened all by itself somehow, outside, by the pool, when they lay on those banana lounges, under the good, dry heat of the California sun.

She was his now.

No need to rush.

The shivering stopped. He pulled back, rubbed his hands up and down her arms, over the nubby fabric of the towel. "Better?"

"Mmm-hmm."

Her mouth was too tempting, tipped up to him like that. He lowered his own, and hesitated, on the brink of the kiss they both hungered for.

She said his name, "Mack," so softly. With such yearning.

He kissed her.

Her mouth was cold, turning warm, and warmer still. The sweetness beyond her lips was as it had been the other day, as he'd remembered for all these years. Incomparable. Perfect. Exactly suited to him.

He slipped his hands under the towel to touch her. Moist and cool. Like satin, her skin. She sighed, and kissed him harder.

They stood there by the door, between the thermostat and the gilt-framed mirror, kissing.

It went on forever, that kiss.

He was the one who pulled away. Gently. Reluctantly. He cupped her chin in both hands and his fingers tangled in the wet strands of her hair. He watched her eyelids open. She looked at him, a dazed and dreamy, utterly relaxed kind of look.

He brought his mouth to hers again. "Are we done with separate rooms, then?" He murmured the words against her soft lips, so that saying them became another kiss.

She smiled, and he felt that smile, her lips moving against his own. "Do you really have to ask?"

"Maybe not. But I'd like to hear you say it."

"It would please you—" each word was a kiss "—to hear me say it?"

"It would please me. Very much."

"Then, yes," she said. "We're done with separate rooms."

She let out a moan that heated the very air around them as he put his mouth against her neck, tangling his fingers in her hair at the same time and pulling her head back to expose her white throat.

He kissed his way down, over the twin points of her collarbone, stopping there briefly to put out his tongue and taste the chlorine and the wonderful smooth sweetness that was her skin.

He took the towel in both hands, peeling it over her shoulders. It dropped with a soft thud to the carpet at their feet. And then he went on, moving down, between the lush curves of her breasts. He pushed at the straps of her suit.

She took his meaning, reaching behind herself, wriggling a little, until she had the top of that white suit unhooked. It fell away and he had her breasts in his hands. They were cool and damp, little goose bumps all over them. He buried his face between them, breathing deeply, remembering....

All the times, their times together. His hands on her body, touching her, kissing her, thinking that she belonged to him, that he could never lose her, that it would always, always be that way.

That they would be together.

Forever.

Together.

He took her nipple into his mouth, drew on it. She surged up toward him, cradling his head in her hands, pulling him nearer, making little hungry, needful sounds, the sounds he remembered.

The sounds he had longed for.

For way too many years.

He let his hands follow her tender curves, down over her torso, under the white waistband of her suit. She shuddered. And then her hands were there, too, helping him to push the thing off and away.

At last she was naked.

Naked in his arms.

He traced a circle around her navel with a lazy finger. She moaned and ground her hips against him. His finger dipped lower, into the soft curls at the apex of her thighs. She lifted herself toward him. He touched her, intimately, feeling the heat and the wetness grow hotter and wetter still at the command of his stroking hand.

She moved against him eagerly as he caressed her. He kissed her other breast, tasted the nipple as it hardened and bloomed. Then he went lower, his mouth sliding down. She put her hands on his shoulders to brace herself—to brace them both—as he sank to his knees before her.

"Mack."

He looked up. And she was looking down, her eyes so dark, the pupils wide-open, her mouth red and full from the kisses they had shared. Her still-wet hair fell in thick coils against her cheeks. She lifted both hands, a languorous movement, swaying on her feet a little, as she smoothed the wet strands back behind her ears. Her full, sweet breasts rose and then settled with the action.

"Mack..." She was still looking down at him.

"Shh..."

"No. No, listen. Mack, outside, by the pool. It was when I realized..."

He laid his hands on the sleek swell of her hips, then slid them inward, so his thumbs met in the warm cove between her thighs.

She gasped. He parted her slowly, gently, sliding his thumbs along the feminine crease beneath those golden curls.

"Glad you came back..." She sighed. "So good...to be with you..." She gasped. "Mack. I did think it was over. I didn't think...there was a chance for us anymore...."

"There's still a chance, Jenna."

"I...I think so, too. Now."

"Good." He leaned closer, scenting her. She moaned,

gave up the effort to talk. She closed her eyes and clutched his shoulders harder.

And he tasted her.

It was something he had feared he might never know again...the taste of her.

He kissed her deeply, using his fingers to part her. She cried out, and then began moving, her hips working, finding the rhythm that would give her the most pleasure. He held her steady as he went on kissing her, drawing on her with his mouth and stroking with his fingers, as well.

"Mack," she groaned, "Oh, Mack...I can't..." She stepped backward. He followed, not letting her go. She found the wall, beside the mirror, to brace herself.

He kept tasting, kissing, stroking. And she surrendered completely at last, with the wall to hold her upright and her hands clutching his head, her body moving of its own volition, seeking the sweet explosion that would give her release.

She cried out again, her head thrown back, as she went over the edge. And he tasted that, too. Felt the tiny nub of her sex pulsing hot against his tongue.

She stiffened, her hips thrust toward him.

And then, slowly, with a low purr of a laugh deep in her throat, she let her knees give way.

Rising, he caught her before she reached the floor. She fell into his arms, soft and limp, no longer shivering, totally his. He turned her without effort, put an arm at her back and one under her knees and lifted her against his chest.

She draped her long, slim arms around his neck and nuzzled his ear. "Where are you taking me?"

"To my bed."

Chapter 11

The walls of Mack's room had been painted a deep maroon. The bed was king-size, with a lush black-and-gold-patterned spread. He had a west-facing window like the one in the main room, looking out on the beach and the harbor beyond. The black-and-gold curtains were open wide and the setting sun hovered, a ball of red fire, above the calm blue sea. The room seemed to burn with light.

Mack laid Jenna on the bed and turned to shut the curtains.

She caught his wrist. "No. Leave it. I like it. It's like being inside a fire."

He looked down at her, his gaze sweeping from her tangled damp hair all the way to her toes. Jenna felt her skin flushing, her nipples tightening, her whole body responding to the heat in that look.

"Inside a fire…" he repeated, as if he found the words arousing.

She rose on the bed, still holding his wrist, until she was kneeling there before him on the black-and-gold coverlet.

She brought his hand to her mouth and kissed the knuckles. Then she ran her own fingers slowly up his arm, as she'd longed to do out by the pool, barely touching the skin, brushing the fine silky hair, making it rise.

He bent forward, kissed her, their lips meeting so lightly, a butterfly of a kiss.

She continued to caress him, sliding her hand past his elbow, over the hard swell of his biceps to his shoulder—and then trailing the pads of her fingers down his side. She smiled when she touched the sensitive skin of his belly and he couldn't manage to hold back a gasp. Slowly, taking all the time in the world about it, she slid a finger under the waistband of his swim trunks. He gasped again.

She pushed her hand farther under and made contact.

A third gasp from him as her hand closed around him. He was so silky, so thick and hard. She smiled to herself. It made her feel powerful to hold him like that, in the palm of her hand.

He muttered a low oath and dispensed with the swim trunks, ruthlessly shoving them down and away.

Now she could touch him freely. And she did, curling her hand more firmly around him, stroking slowly, loving the feel of him, loving the way he closed his eyes and threw his head back, a deep moan escaping his parted lips.

She bent closer, lowered her mouth to him and took

him inside. He shuddered. She loved that, had always loved that, the feel of his big body shaking at her touch.

He allowed her a few minutes of that kind of play. Then he caught her face in his hands and made her look up at him.

"No more." His voice was ragged. "I'll lose it."

She couldn't resist. She bent one more time, gave him one last, lingering kiss, one he bore in a breath-held, agonized silence.

Then she raised her gaze to his again. "Come down to me."

He didn't move, only looked at her, a look that burned like the light from the slowly sinking sun, a look that claimed her. She shivered a little, but not with cold.

She took his right hand, tugged on it. "Mack…"

With his left hand, he reached for the drawer in the nightstand and came out with a small foil-wrapped pouch.

Jenna stared at the pouch and remembered.

Mack had always used protection.

Because he did not want to make a baby.

She closed her eyes, old hurts rising.

"Jenna." He said her name so gently.

She kept her eyes closed, despising herself a little for her own reaction. She was not the lost and confused young woman she had once been, the woman who had begged for a baby to fill the emptiness in her life.

It was totally appropriate that he'd have protection. Totally appropriate and right.

And really, what would she have done if he hadn't shown a little forethought here, since she wasn't on the Pill and she'd failed to pack a diaphragm? Would she have pushed him away at the last minute? Or worse, taken a foolish, thoughtless chance and possibly ended up pregnant, when nothing between them was settled or sure?

She opened her eyes, gave him a smile. A real smile, though perhaps it did quiver a little at the corners. "I see you're prepared."

"Did you think I wouldn't be?"

"I guess I didn't think about it either way. Until now."

"I made no secret of wanting you, Jenna."

"No. No, of course you didn't. You did the right thing, to be ready when the moment came. This is just…old stuff I'm reacting to, that's all."

His eyes narrowed briefly. She knew that he understood exactly what "old stuff" she meant. But he didn't speak of it.

She sighed.

He was staring down at her. Waiting, still clearly aroused, but holding himself tightly in check. The light in the room was redder, deeper, as the sun touched the ocean at the edge of the world.

"Do you want to stop?" he asked, his voice rough, dangerous—yet at the same time rigidly controlled.

She pressed her lips together, drew in a breath and shook her head.

Another surge of heat flared in his eyes. And then his face changed, the look of strain passing, leaving his hard features softer.

He tore open the foil pouch.

She held out her hand. "Let me."

He said her name then, softly, hungrily, with a needful tenderness that brought tears to shimmer in her eyes and made everything suddenly all right again.

He set the torn pouch in her palm. She peeled it open to reveal the condom inside. Then slowly, lovingly, she rolled it down over him.

She set the empty pouch on the nightstand and held out her hand again. This time he took it, coming down onto the bed with her, straddling her, reaching for her other arm and raising them both above her head.

He held her there, in that vulnerable position, rising up enough to slip his legs between hers and then kneeling at the juncture of her open thighs.

He bent close, kissed the soft whiteness at the underside of each upraised arm. She moaned, lifting her torso. After a moment of sweetest agony, he gave her what she wanted, his mouth closing hot and strong over a nipple. She moaned again, and pushed herself toward his suckling kiss.

He drew deep. She felt the pull, down in the female heart of her. She wanted to reach for him, to drag him down and take him inside her.

But he continued to hold her arms helpless over her head, as he went on kissing her breast, drawing so deeply that she thought she might faint from the sheer erotic pull.

She couldn't bear it.

Yet she did bear it.

And bore it some more when he turned his attention to the other breast.

At last, long after the point when she felt absolutely certain she could bear it no longer, his mouth went roaming. He trailed one endless wet kiss over the top swell of her breast, up to her neck, her throat, her jaw, her cheek...

He sank down upon her as his mouth covered hers.

She opened for him, rising toward him as he filled her. They cried out together.

Perfect, yes. Exactly right.

Even after all these years.

They began to move together, finding the old rhythms instinctively, with no thought or effort required. She wrapped her legs around him and they were one, in the red, burning light of the slowly setting sun.

She felt his pleasure cresting. Her completion rose to meet it. They hit the peak together on an endless, seeking kiss.

Jenna realized she must have slept.

The sun had set long ago, the red glow slowly fading to darkness. Now the room was silver and shadows. She lifted her head. Out the window, the night sky looked hazy, the stars bled away in the gleam of harbor lights.

Mack lay almost on top of her, his cheek against her breast and an arm across her waist. She looked down at his head, dark in the half-light, and she smiled a woman's knowing smile.

He stirred, as if he felt her looking at him. She wanted to touch him. Maybe she should have let him sleep some more. But the reality of having him here where she could put her hand on him was too tempting to resist.

So she ran a finger around the whorling shape of his ear.

He lifted his head and opened droopy eyes.

Then he smiled. And she smiled right back—just

the kind of smiles they had given each other nine years before, the first night they met, when they'd ended up right where they were now: in bed together. That night, she remembered, Byron had jumped on the mattress between them, settled himself in and purred so loudly that they had both laughed.

Mack touched her cheek with a finger and guided a swatch of hair back behind her ear. "You're frowning. Why?"

"I miss Byron. I wish he were here."

He chuckled. "I don't know. The way I remember it, he always took up more than his fair share of the bed."

She idly traced a figure eight on the hard bulge of muscle at his shoulder. "I hope he's doing all right. He needs companionship, and I have this feeling that Lacey might be leaving him alone too much."

"I'm sure he's fine." He kissed her chin.

A question occurred to her. And now that she'd truly given herself to this two-week endeavor, she felt perfectly easy in her mind about asking it.

"Mack?"

He rolled to his back, then turned his head to lift an eyebrow at her. "What?"

"Why did you fight me so hard over Byron—and then all of a sudden just decide to let it go?"

He turned his face to the ceiling and put his arm across his eyes. Unease tightened her stomach. Was he going to evade, or maybe become angry with her for bringing up an unpleasant part of their past?

He dropped his arm and met her eyes again. He didn't look angry at all. The tightness in her stomach faded away. "Hey. I had a real soft spot for that damn cat. And I considered him mine as much as he was yours."

"I know. But those aren't the real reasons you tried to take him from me, are they?"

He was watching the shadows on the ceiling again. A silent moment passed before he answered. "The 'real' reasons aren't so simple. They're angry reasons, and they're vengeful. I'm not proud to admit to them."

"Please. I just want to understand."

His chest rose and fell as he drew a deep breath. "I don't know. Sometimes I think that honesty between the sexes has been highly overrated."

She realized he was teasing her. She nudged him in the side. "Come on. Tell me."

He rolled over, lifted himself up on his elbows and stared at the headboard, which was an interesting creation of dark wood and wrought iron. "I didn't want to let you go," he said, "but I knew you weren't coming back to me. And I was damn insulted that you wouldn't take any alimony. I'd worked my tail off to make a decent living—and the price, I was beginning to realize, had been losing you. It seemed to me that the least you could do was take some of the money, ease my pride a little. That way I could have told myself that at least I'd been good to you financially. But you wouldn't take any money. All you wanted was the cat."

She touched his back, starting at the swell of his shoulder and running her hand downward, over hard muscle and tight skin. "So you decided you wouldn't let me have him."

"That's right. But after a year of the old back-and-forth, demands and counterdemands from your lawyer and then mine, I started to see it a little bit differently."

She suggested, "You mean you realized you were acting like an ass?"

He leaned closer, kissed the tip of her nose. "Exactly. And I told my lawyer to get it over with, that you could have the cat."

She dared to ask the next meaningful question. "So then, if you wanted to get it over with, why didn't you sign the papers?"

He let out a long breath. "I thought we'd been through that one. I didn't sign the papers because I didn't really want a divorce from you, not subconsciously, anyway. Your lawyer worked up the settlement and sent it to my lawyer—who was a colleague of mine, by the way, someone who worked in the firm, which I left shortly after you and I came to terms."

"Because of the class-action suit?"

"Right. The firm wouldn't touch it. But I knew I could win it and that it would pay off big. So I left the firm. And when the divorce papers came through, my lawyer got hold of me and told me to come in and sign them. I never got around to it. I was too busy with the lawsuit, getting what I'd always wanted, making myself into a millionaire—or that's what I told myself. I paid my lawyer off and, periodically, his assistant would call me to remind me to come in. In the end, I went and got those papers, thinking that I'd take care of them myself. But I didn't. I stuck them in a drawer and told myself I'd forgotten about them."

He glanced directly at her, saw her disbelieving expression and added, "Just as I'm sure you told yourself you didn't notice that the final decree never happened to come through. But, as I have pointed out before, I think you did notice. And you didn't do anything about it, either. Not for all these years."

She acquiesced. "Maybe you're right."

"Whew." He pretended to wipe his brow. "I think we're making progress here."

"So do I. And I want us to continue to make progress." She touched the side of his face, which was slightly rough now with evening stubble. "I have another question. A request, really. And before I ask it, I want to say that I promise you, I do intend to stay with you for the remainder of our two weeks. I *want* these two weeks now. I hope you believe me."

She saw in his eyes that he knew what was coming. He moved back to his own pillow. "Damn it, Jenna."

She didn't allow his retreat, but canted up on an elbow so that she could wrap her hand around the back of his neck. She rubbed, gently but insistently. "Mack…"

He gave her a measuring, wary look. "You want the divorce papers, don't you?"

She leaned closer and kissed his rough cheek. "I do, Mack. And I want them now."

Chapter 12

He rolled away from her, brought his feet to the floor and rose to loom over her. "Why?"

She sat and plumped her pillow against the headboard. Then she reached for the sheet and pulled it over herself. "I want us to start fresh, Mack. You don't need to hold those papers over my head anymore to get me to be with you. Please. Just give them up."

He stared down at her. He had on his lawyer look now. Calculating. Distant. "You don't need them until our two weeks are over."

She ached for him then, for that part of him that still couldn't quite trust her good intentions, the part of him, she realized now, that always expected to be abandoned in the end.

"You're right," she said. "I don't need the papers right now. But I do need for you to *give* them to me now."

He asked again, "Why?"

She phrased her answer with care. "You agreed to certain things, Mack. First, that you would sign those papers five and half years ago. And then, a few weeks ago, that you would sign them and send them to me. Those were…promises, Mack. Promises you broke. I think you owe it to me to do what you can now to make good on those promises. I think you owe it to yourself."

A muscle worked in his jaw. "What about the first promise? The one we made to each other. *To have and to hold,* damn it. What about that?"

"The time came when we both agreed we couldn't keep that promise anymore."

"Not for me it didn't. You were the one who left."

Patience, she thought. She raked her tangled hair away from her face and kept her voice calm and low. "Yes, Mack. I did leave. And you may be right that we both knew we weren't…finished with each other. But I also believe there was a time when we both accepted that our marriage had ended."

"I didn't," he said. "I never accepted that, not really."

She reached out and caught his hand. He didn't pull away. She decided to consider that a good sign. "Come back to bed. I didn't want this to end up a battle. I honestly didn't." She lifted the sheet with her free hand. "Please?"

His jaw remained set, his eyes cool and wary—but he allowed her to pull him back to the bed. Using the hand that wasn't holding his, she propped his pillow against the headboard for him and then settled the sheet over them both.

"It was over, Mack. You know it was."

He looked down at their joined hands. "What is this? You just have to be right about this, is that it?"

"No. I'm only trying to convince you to do what you know in your heart is the fair and best thing."

He squeezed her hand—and not gently. "Don't try to tell me what's in my own damn heart."

"Mack. Let's look at this another way."

He slid her a suspicious glance. "What other way?"

She sucked in a breath and took another big leap into even more dangerous territory. "Tell me this. Have you made love with any other women since we've been apart?"

He turned toward her then. His eyes gleamed through the dark, feral and a little frightening. "Your point being?"

"My point being that I know you took your wedding vows seriously. You would not have slept with someone else unless you believed at the time that you weren't married to me anymore."

They stared at each other. Jenna's heart drummed in her own ears. She felt like a woman who'd decided to stroll across a swamp—using alligator backs as stepping-stones.

Mack asked softly, "Did *you?* Make love with anyone else?"

She knew for certain then that there had been other women. Strangely, the knowledge caused her no more than a twinge of sad regret. Whom he'd slept with in the time they'd been apart was his business. Jenna truly believed what she was trying to make him see: they *had* been divorced—in their hearts, anyway. She only hoped that his lovers had been good to him, and that he had treated them well in return.

"No, Mack. I didn't make love with anyone else, but not because I felt I was still married. I *was* divorced from you. I just…never found anyone else I wanted that way."

"Not even the good doctor?"

"No. Not even Logan." She waited, almost wishing she hadn't taken the argument in that particular direction.

He looked straight ahead, toward the door to the main room. "You make me ashamed."

"I swear to you, that was not my intention."

He gave her hand another quick, hard squeeze. She squeezed back.

He said, "You'll have to let go—if you want me to get those damn papers from my suitcase."

She did let go. And he went into the walk-in closet in the corner of the room. When he came out again, he was carrying a large manila envelope. He sat on the edge of the bed and opened it, then pulled the papers out. "Look them over. They're signed and notarized."

"I trust you," she said.

He chuckled at that, and ruefully shook his head. Then he shoved everything back into the envelope and handed it to her.

"Go on," he said. "Put it away."

She canted forward and kissed him. "Thank you."

"Go ahead. Do it."

She pushed back the sheet and left the bed, strolling nude to the door, through the main room and into her part of the suite. There, she tucked the envelope into a side pocket of one of her suitcases.

When she returned to him, he had slid beneath the

sheet and leaned up against the headboard again. He watched her walk toward him.

"You look good, Jenna."

She smiled her pleasure at the compliment as she pulled back the sheet and got in beside him.

"Are you hungry?" he asked. "It's after nine."

She shook her head. "Not right now. You?"

"Not really."

She felt his hand brush her thigh. She cuddled up closer, rested her head against his chest. "It's been a long time."

"Too damn long." He put his hand beneath her chin and guided it up so that their lips could meet.

The small funeral chapel was filled with flowers.

There were arrangements on stands, in tall vases, in baskets and in urns. Doreen's especial favorite had been white roses, so two giant vases of them flanked the open casket. Unlike most hothouse blooms, they actually gave off a scent.

"Lovely," Lois said. "The smell of those roses…"

"Dory would be pleased," Alec added in a tight voice.

Inside the open casket, Doreen Henderson McGarrity Telford lay in a bed of white satin, her tiny, thin hands resting on her stomach. She wore a trim blue suit with a slim knee-length skirt. The short jacket had three-quarter sleeves and a round collar. A little round hat with a half veil sat daintily atop her graying chestnut-brown hair.

During the viewing, which preceded the funeral ceremony, Jenna stared down at Doreen's small, serene face, thinking that she looked like a nice, aging housewife from an earlier era, a nice housewife who had lain down for a nap in her favorite suit.

Jenna sat with Mack and Alec and Lois in the front row. The chapel was small, and only about a third full.

"Mostly people from the agency," Alec whispered. "The people we worked with. And a few neighbors, of course..."

During the viewing and before the service began, the others approached and offered their sympathies. Alec nodded and thanked them and told them how grateful he was that they could come.

The service was brief, a few hymns and hopeful verses from the Bible and some kind words from a robust, florid-faced minister. Once the last prayer had been said, the minister invited them all to proceed to the cemetery.

In the cemetery, the pallbearers carried the casket from the long limousine to the place that had been prepared for it, beneath the feathery green leaves of a jacaranda tree. Come June and July, the branches would be weighted with soft violet blooms. Jenna closed her eyes and pictured that, the masses of purple flowers arching over the cool, grassy spot. She found the image soothing.

Once the pallbearers had set the casket in place, the minister quoted more scripture and said another prayer. Alec placed a single white rose on the closed lid of the coffin.

And then it was over.

Lois whispered, "We're all going to the house."

Jenna nodded. Mack took her hand and they turned for the car.

At Alec's house there were cookies and cake and

punch on the table. People stood in little groups and talked quietly, of what a nice service it had been, so simple and moving. They said fond things about Doreen, how quiet she'd always been, and so good at heart. Alec made a point of introducing Mack around, and of explaining how pleased and grateful he was that Dory's son had come to help him through this difficult time.

If people were surprised to find that Doreen had a son, they didn't show it. Watching their faces, Jenna thought that they really *weren't* surprised. It seemed to her that they simply hadn't known Doreen well enough to feel that her son was someone they should have been told about.

And why was that? Jenna wondered. Had Doreen kept people at a distance in order to minimize the possibility that the question of whether she had children would ever come up? Or was it, perhaps, just that Doreen was a very private sort of person?

Jenna wished it might be the latter, but feared the former.

How many different ways, she wondered, had Doreen paid for the choice she'd made to give her children away?

Jenna looked for Mack and found him across the room, talking quietly to Lois. He glanced up and their gazes met. Jenna let the wonderful jolt of awareness sizzle through her, watching as a smile teased the corners of his mouth.

She thought of the night before and felt acutely alive, all her nerves humming, her skin prickling. Was it wrong to feel so wonderful on the day they laid Mack's mother in the ground?

She didn't think so. And she didn't think that Doreen would have minded at all—though of course, she'd never know.

People began leaving around six. Jenna and Mack stayed until everyone else had left. Then they, too, said their goodbyes. Mack explained that the two of them had a morning flight to Miami.

Lois said she was staying for another week or two, and then she would try to talk Alec into coming and visiting her in Phoenix for a while.

Alec said, "Mack, when you talk to your sisters, please tell them I hope someday to meet them."

Mack glanced away, then back. "It might be a while, Alec."

Alec squeezed his arm. "Whenever you get around to it, then."

"Fair enough. You know how to reach me if you ever need me for anything."

"Yes, of course. I have that address and phone number you gave Dory."

"That should do it."

"Mack?"

"Yeah?"

"It's meant so much—that you were here."

Mack cleared his throat and nodded. The two men looked at each other, each seeming to have something more to say, but neither actually getting the words out.

"Go on." Lois elbowed her brother in the ribs. "Give him a hug. You know you want to."

Lois's prompting was all Alec needed. He reached out and put his thin arms around Mack. Mack returned the embrace, but awkwardly, as if a hug was something he wasn't quite sure he ought to be participating in.

Finally Alec took Mack by the arms and stepped back. "You're a fine man, son. Dory was so proud of you…and so am I."

Mack mumbled something. It might have been "Thank you."

Alec's eyes gleamed with held-back tears as he turned to Jenna. She grabbed him and hugged him hard. He whispered, "I hope things work out between you two."

She pulled back, gave him a nod and a smile, then turned to Lois to get one more hug.

"Don't be strangers. Stay in touch," Lois commanded as she let them out the door.

"You okay?" Jenna asked softly when she and Mack were in the Lincoln, headed back to the hotel.

He felt for her hand, found it. "I'm okay. Ready to get out of here, ready to hang out under the banyan trees, to watch a Key West sunset from the deck of *The Shady Deal*."

"That's the name of your boat? *The Shady Deal?*"

"That's right."

She lifted their joined hands and kissed the back of his. "I never pictured you living in a place like Key West."

He gave her a quick grin, then focused on the street ahead of them again. "I love it. It's tropical. And it's seedy. It has very little dignity. But it has style. It's the perfect place for me."

"Mack McGarrity. You are never seedy. No way."

"Hah. But you admit I lack dignity."

"I didn't say that."

"But you thought it."

"I did not."

He had to pull his hand away to make a turn. She watched his profile, saw his expression grow serious.

"What are you thinking?"

"So strange," he said. "Those people today, coming up to me, offering their condolences. Condolences for what? I never really knew her."

"It's what people do at funerals, Mack. A show of support, letting you know that they care."

"I understand that. I only meant that it felt strange. I kept thinking, Who *was* she, anyway? What in the hell went on in her mind?"

"I think…she was a good woman, at heart. That she made a tough choice, told a big lie to someone she loved and then never knew how to tell the one she loved the truth."

Mack laughed, a sound without humor. "I guess we can think whatever the hell we want now, can't we? She won't be around to tell us we're wrong."

"She was a good woman, Mack, I just know she was. After all, Alec loved her. A man like Alec could only love someone good…and I know that she loved you. I'm positive of it."

He sent her another glance, a glance with doubt in it, and the shadow of a lifelong hurt. But he didn't say anything. Not much later, they reached the hotel.

The minute they got inside the suite, Mack pulled her close and buried his head against the curve of her neck. She wrapped her arms around him, held him as tightly as he was holding her.

His lips moved against her neck as his hands fumbled at the few pins she'd used to hold up her hair. He found the pins, dropped them.

Her hair fell around her shoulders. "There," he whispered. "Yeah…"

She tipped her head back, offering her lips. His mouth covered hers.

Jenna gave herself up to his kiss, understanding his need right then—to touch, to feel, to reach out for life. She moaned as his tongue mated with hers.

He began to undress her, sustaining the kiss as he walked her toward his room. They left a trail of clothing through the main room, into his room, to the edge of the bed. They had to break apart to remove the rest: his shoes and socks and boxer briefs, her panty hose and bra.

He reached for the drawer in the nightstand and took out a condom. She rolled it down over him. They fell across the bed together.

Jenna ended up on top. When she took him inside her, they both kept their eyes open. The curtains were closed then, the room dim and cool. She moved above him, looking down, wishing she could take all his old hurts into herself and turn them to pure joy.

He surged up inside her. She felt him pulsing, finding release. She didn't try to reach a climax of her own, but simply let herself relax on top of him, cuddling her head into the crook of his shoulder, smiling to herself as his arms came around her.

She turned her head, pressed her lips against the side of his neck. "It was a tough day."

He made a low, lazy sound of agreement. His hand was stroking her hair.

"And we'll be in Florida tomorrow…" she reminded

him tenderly. "We'll spend the rest of our two weeks doing whatever you want to do."

"Hmm. Whatever I want?"

She nipped the place she'd kissed a moment before. "Don't push your luck."

They were still in bed an hour later when the phone rang. Mack answered it, then handed the phone to Jenna.

"It's your sister."

Jenna took it. "Lacey?"

"Oh, God, Jenna." Lacey sounded as if she might burst into tears. "Please don't hate me...."

"Hate you? Lacey, what are you talking about?"

"It's Byron," her sister said. "He ran away. I don't have a clue where he's gone."

Chapter 13

"Byron's missing?" Jenna held back her own cry of dismay. She thought of the strange way her sister had sounded the last time they had spoken. "How long has it been since you saw him?"

"Wednesday. He was here then, I swear to you."

"So he disappeared...?"

"Yesterday. I came back to the house to feed him and I couldn't find him."

"Have you checked all the closets? And the cupboards in the kitchen? Sometimes he—"

"I swear to you, Jenna. I've looked everywhere, into every cupboard, every closet, every nook and cranny. He must have gotten out somehow, though I can't figure out how he managed it. None of the screens are unhooked, and I never left any of the doors open." Lacey let out a moan. "I know what you're thinking. And you're right. I didn't pay enough attention to him. I've been having…well, the last few days have been… Let's just say I haven't been around the house much."

"What's going on? Where have you been?"

"Oh, Jen. It's…I think we'd better talk about that later. Right now, there's more you have to know."

Jenna slumped against the headboard, "There is?"

"Mmm-hmm. You see, today I…I thought I heard him, in the attic…." Lacey paused long enough to let out another small moan of misery.

Jenna sat up a little straighter. "You thought you heard Byron in the attic?"

"Yes."

"And?"

"I went up there."

"And?"

"I thought I heard him again, way over in the corner, under the eaves—you know, above the upstairs bedroom in the front of the house?"

"Yes. I know the place you mean."

"There's no attic floor there, just those big beams and the ceiling of the bedroom below and—"

Jenna was getting the picture. "You didn't…"

"I did. I put my foot through the bedroom ceiling. I smashed up the bone in my heel, 'mushroomed' it. That's what the doctor said. And I also left a big, ragged hole in the ceiling. You should see it. What a mess."

"Forget about the ceiling for now. What about you? How did you get back down out of the attic?"

"It wasn't pretty. But I managed it."

"And then?"

"I called 911 and they came and they carted me over to Meadow Valley Memorial. When I got there, they took X-rays, wrapped up my foot and gave me some crutches. They sent me home for the night, but I have to be back tomorrow by two in the afternoon. For surgery." Lacey moaned some more. "Oh, I didn't want to call you. But I figured I'd better. I'm going to have trouble getting over to the shop to check on the money. And then there's Byron..."

"You say you're at home now?"

"Yes. Until tomorrow."

"Is someone there to help you?"

"Mira and Maud were here." Lacey spoke of the "terrible twins," her friends from high school. "They made me some dinner and a bed downstairs. Mira said she'd be back tomorrow to take me to the hospital."

"So you're all right. For tonight?"

"Yes, yes, I'm fine. I can get around on the crutches if I have to, and they gave me some painkillers, so it doesn't hurt too much."

"I'll be there tomorrow, as soon as I can get a flight."

"Oh, God. I've ruined everything. Jenna, I'm so sorry for messing up like this. And poor Byron... He *has* to turn up soon. I just know it. He's probably off somewhere sulking, don't you think? Oh, I feel so guilty. I feel like a real jerk...."

"Don't worry. I'll see you tomorrow, I promise."

"Mack McGarrity will probably hire a hit man to do me in."

Jenna glanced at Mack, who was lying on his side facing her, his head propped on his hand. He'd been frowning since he'd heard that Byron was missing— and he'd started scowling at the point where Jenna mentioned getting a flight.

Now he demanded, "What the hell is going on?"

Jenna waved at him for silence and spoke to her

sister again. "I mean it. Stop worrying. I'll be there. Probably not tonight. It's too late. But tomorrow, as early as I can."

"All right. I am so sorry."

"Relax. I'll see you soon."

Lacey murmured a pitiful goodbye and Jenna hung up.

Mack pulled himself to a sitting position and folded his arms across his chest. "Well?"

She hit him with it. "Byron's missing and Lacey broke her foot. I have to go back to Meadow Valley right away."

Mack said nothing.

He was thinking that the damn cat would eventually come back on his own. Bub knew how to take care of himself. He'd been a stray when he'd suckered Jenna and Mack into adopting him.

And didn't Lacey have a few friends in her hometown who could help her through the next few days?

But he could tell by the look in Jenna's eyes and the set of her soft, very kissable mouth that she was going. No sense getting on her bad side trying to talk her out of it. He'd worked damn hard, after all, to get himself on her good side. And he really liked it there.

"Mack." She looked adorably contrite. "I'm so sorry. Your two weeks in paradise don't seem to be turning out the way you planned."

"I'm going with you."

"Are you sure? We could—"

He didn't let her even suggest an alternative. "I said I'm going with you."

"All right. If you're positive that's what you want to do."

* * *

They arrived at Sacramento Executive Airport at 10:00 a.m. the next morning. Mack had a rental car, another Lexus, waiting and ready to go.

It was a little after eleven when they reached the house at the top of West Broad Street in Meadow Valley. Mack pulled in behind a dark blue Cadillac.

He turned to Jenna. "Looks like your sister's got company."

Jenna gulped. "Yes. That's Logan's car."

Mack turned off the engine. "What's he doing here?"

"I don't know. I suppose he heard that Lacey was hurt. He's always thought of himself as a kind of big brother to her. I'd imagine he just wanted to check on her, to see that she's all right."

Mack didn't look the least satisfied with her suggested explanation. "You think he knows you're coming back today?"

Jenna let out a long, exasperated sigh. "I don't have the faintest idea what Logan knows about all this."

"I don't like it."

"Can we just go in, please? We can't learn anything sitting out here."

"Fine."

Jenna met Mack at the rear of the car and took the two bags he handed her. They trooped up the front walk, Jenna in the lead.

On the porch, Jenna set down her bags, anchored her purse strap more securely on her shoulder and unlocked the door. Then she stuck her head in and called out good and loud, "Hello? Lacey?"

After an unnerving three beats of silence, Lacey answered, "We're back here!"

Jenna turned to Mack, who stood on the porch behind her, holding a suitcase in one hand and a garment bag slung over the opposite shoulder. "They're in the back parlor."

He shrugged.

She thought of Logan, of the way the unshed tears had gleamed in his dark eyes the last time they'd spoken. Guilt gave her a sharp, very unpleasant little poke.

"Jenna. Are we going in?"

"Of course."

"Well?"

"All right." She pushed the door open all the way, picked up the bags again and entered the house. "Just, um, set everything down here."

They lined the suitcases up to the left of the door and Mack draped the garment bag over them. Then there was nothing else to do but seek out her sister and Logan in the back of the house. "This way."

Mack followed behind her, along the central hall to the back parlor.

They found Lacey sitting in the old velvet easy chair, her injured foot propped on an ottoman in front of her, with pillows stacked up to keep the foot high. A set of crutches lay on the hardwood floor beside the chair. And a TV tray sat on the other side, laden with tissues and a water glass, a thick paperback novel, the remote telephone and a bottle of some kind of prescription medicine.

Logan stood by the fireplace. He was a long way from tears right then. His strong jaw was set and his dark eyes glittered with what looked like anger. Lacey seemed upset, as well. Two vivid spots of color stained her pale cheeks.

No one spoke for an agonizing three or four seconds. The silence seemed to bounce off the cream-colored walls. Jenna cast a glance at Mack, watched him eyeing both her sister and Logan.

Then Lacey declared way too brightly, "You're early!"

Jenna frowned. "Not really." She had called Lacey from the airport and told her that they'd be about an hour.

"Well, I mean, I didn't expect… It's just that I…" Lacey waved a hand. "Oh, never mind. Um, hello, Mack. How have you been?"

"Just fine."

"You remember…each other?" Lacey put out a hand palm up and gestured from Mack to Logan.

The two men exchanged curt, unsmiling nods.

Lacey looked at her outstretched hand as if she didn't remember how it had gotten extended. She brought it back and made a pretense of smoothing her hair. "Um, Logan heard I had hurt myself. He just came to check on me." Her big smile got bigger and her cheeks colored even more deeply. "Didn't you, Logan?"

Logan hesitated, but then said gruffly, "That's right." He turned and spoke to Jenna. "She's got Jeb Leventhal as her surgeon. He's the best. She'll be fine."

Jenna gave him a smile that was probably as false as Lacey's. "That's good to hear."

Logan cleared his throat. "Well. I think it's time I was going."

"Yes." Lacey's eagerness was painful to see. "You'd better go."

Logan nodded at Mack again. And for the second time, Mack nodded back. Logan smiled at Jenna. She smiled in return.

Lord, this was awful. All four of them, smiling and nodding, their sentences trailing off into harrowing silences.

At last Logan turned and left them.

No one said a word until they heard the front door close. By then, Lacey's smile had slipped. She sighed.

Jenna went to her, brushed the soft, wild curls away from her face and placed a kiss at her temple. "Are you in pain? Is there anything I can get you?"

"No. I'm fine. I mean, it hurts, but I just took a codeine half an hour ago. I'm all right." She bit her lower lip. "Byron hasn't shown up yet."

"He will. Soon. I'm sure."

"I'm such a—"

"Lace. Ease up on yourself, will you?"

"I went ahead and slept down here." She indicated the convertible sofa a few feet away, which was folded out into a bed, the covers all tangled, testimony to an uneasy night. "It's just too hard to get up and down the stairs."

"We might as well move you into my room." Jenna had the master suite on the ground floor at the front of the house.

"No. I'm okay here. I'll only feel more rotten if I kick you out of your own bed."

"Lacey, it's all right, really. There are three bedrooms upstairs. I can take one of them, no problem."

"Right. Maybe the one with the gaping, ragged hole in the ceiling."

"Stop it. A hole in the ceiling is not that big a deal."

"Keep your room. I mean it. And will you just quit fussing over me? Please?" Lacey cast a glance at Mack, who waited, arms folded across his chest, near the stairs that led to the upper floor. "Are you staying, Mack?"

"I am."

"Then tell my sister that she should help you bring in your suitcases or something, will you?"

One side of his mouth kicked up. "Jenna. You should help me bring in our suitcases. Or something."

Jenna sent an exasperated glance from her sister to Mack and then back to Lacey.

Lacey waved her hand again. "Go on. You two get your stuff inside. I'm fine." She picked up the phone from the TV tray at her side. "I'll just call Mira and tell her she won't have to ferry me to the hospital, after all."

"Give a yell if you—"

Lacey was already punching up numbers. "I will, I will. Now, go on. Please."

Jenna led Mack back to the front door. But once she had both bags in her hands, she just stood there, undecided.

Mack read her easily. "I'll share your room," he said. "And your bed. I doubt that your sister is going to be shocked if she finds out."

She turned and led him where he wanted to go, to the door halfway back down the central hall that opened onto her bed-sitting room and adjoining bath.

"I like this," he said, setting the suitcase down on the russet-and-saffron-colored rug and laying the garment bag over a chair. He glanced around approvingly at the dark furniture, the pale walls and the red velvet comforter on the wide four-poster bed.

Her heart was beating way too fast, knocking itself painfully against the wall of her chest.

Somehow, she felt so terribly…vulnerable, here, with him, in this particular room, the room that had once been her parents' room and later her mother's alone. The room that, for the past few years, had become her own private retreat.

Strange. She'd paraded before him in their Long Beach hotel suite without a stitch to cover herself and found it as easy and natural as breathing. But standing here with him now, fully clothed, their suitcases between them, she felt utterly naked and extremely uncomfortable about it.

"I'll…clear out a couple of drawers for you. And there's room in the closet for whatever you need to hang up. Why don't you go on out and bring the rest of the bags in and I'll—"

"Jenna." His voice was like velvet. His eyes knew too much.

"I… What?"

He stepped around the suitcases and came up close. Too close. He lifted a hand and touched her, his finger burning a caress into the tender skin of her cheek. "Your upper lip is quivering."

"Twitching, you mean."

"Twitching. Right. Nervous?"

"I… Yes. For some reason I am."

"You never thought I'd be in this room with you, did you?"

That was true. She hadn't. Not ever.

But she had dreamed of him often while she slept beneath the red comforter. Dreams like the one where they floated on the white bed, naked without ever removing their clothes…

His hand trailed downward, over her jaw, tracing a heated line along the side of her throat.

"Mack…"

"What? Afraid I'll push you back on that nice, big bed and have my way with you right now?"

She caught his hand before it could go any farther, and then kissed it, a gesture they both recognized as placating. "It's just… It is strange. Having you here. You only came here with me that one other time, remember?"

"Our first Christmas together. We slept in that room upstairs in the back."

"My room. Or it was until my mother died." She let go of his hand. "You hated Meadow Valley."

He didn't try to deny it. "I was afraid you were going to try to trap me here—and don't get that look. For me, at that time, moving here would have been a trap. And you kept dropping hints, remember? About how I could start my first law practice here, hang out a shingle over on Commercial Street. It wasn't what I had in mind for myself."

"I know. You were headed for a partnership in a major big-city firm."

"And all you wanted was to come back to your hometown."

"That's right."

"And in the end, you did come back, didn't you?"

"Yes. I did."

"And something else is bothering you, beyond my being here in this room with you, beyond unhappy memories of the way we were. What is it?"

She leaned on the end of the bed and rested her cheek against one of the tall, carved posts. "I just feel strange about this whole thing, I guess. Coming back here, instead of going to Key West. Running into Logan again. And something's going on with Lacey, did you notice? Something other than her broken foot and Byron's disappearance."

He gave her a shrug and the slightest hint of a smile.

She frowned at him. "What? You know something I don't?"

"It's only a guess."

"Tell me."

"It looks to me like your ex-fiancé has moved beyond the big-brother role with your little sister."

"Moved beyond the…?" Her mouth dropped open. She shut it. "You mean…? No. Not those two. Never in a million years. Lacey said she might check on him, you know, to see that he was all right, after you and I left town, but…"

"Looks to me like she checked on him but good. And I have to tell you, I think it's great. Whatever distracts the good doctor from his lifelong devotion to you is A-okay with me."

Jenna could not get her mind around such an idea. "But Mack…Logan and Lacey? I just can't see it."

Mack shrugged. "My other suitcase and your overnight case are still in the trunk. I'll get them."

Jenna stared rather blindly after him as he went out the door into the hall.

Imagine that. Logan and Lacey. Could it be true?

She'd have to ask Lacey…when the right opportunity presented itself, of course. After Lacey had made it through her surgery, sometime when the two of them were alone.

Jenna was still standing in the same spot when Mack returned with the rest of their bags. The sight of him got her moving. She went to the big bureau to empty a couple of drawers.

Lacey's surgery went well. She had to stay in the hospital that night, but Dr. Leventhal promised she could go home Sunday morning.

Mack and Jenna left the hospital at a little after seven. At the house, Jenna found enough in the cupboards and refrigerator to fix them a simple meal of pasta and salad. She even had a nice bottle of red wine she'd been saving.

They cleaned up the kitchen together. And then they went to her bedroom.

By then, the feeling of strangeness at having Mack with her in the house where she'd grown up had passed. She found it all felt very natural between them again. Natural and right and more beautiful than ever. They made love slowly, making the pleasure last.

Afterward, they soaked in the claw-footed tub in her bathroom. She sat between his legs and leaned back against his chest.

"This is heaven." She sighed.

He murmured his agreement, his hands busy below the surface of the water, doing things that very soon had her moaning and calling his name.

Eventually they retired to the four-poster bed again and dropped off to sleep around midnight.

It was after two when Jenna woke. She lay staring at

the ceiling, certain she had heard the low, rusty sound of Byron's peculiar meow.

No other cat meowed like her cat. He did it so seldom. It always came out rough and raspy, as if his vocal cords had forgotten how to make the right sound.

There it was again.

Jenna sat up in bed.

Mack turned over and squinted at her through the darkness. "Huh?"

"I thought I heard Byron. You know that meow he has? Kind of raspy and rough?"

He sat up beside her, instantly awake. "Where?"

She was already pushing back the covers. "I'm not sure. Outside the bedroom door, I think. In the hall."

The shirt Mack had been wearing the day before lay over a chair. She scooped it up and pulled it on. It covered her to the tops of her thighs. Hardly modest, but it *was* just the two of them—and maybe, if they were lucky, one raspy-voiced black cat.

Mack took a minute to yank on his boxer shorts. Then he followed her out into the hall.

Jenna switched on the light. Nothing.

"Could we just look around?" she asked.

He shrugged. "Why not?"

They searched the two parlors, the kitchen and laundry room, even the bathroom under the stairs.

"Let's go ahead and check upstairs," she suggested when they'd exhausted all the possibilities on the lower floor. Mack didn't argue, so she turned on the light at the foot of stairs and they started up. At the top, she crossed the landing and entered the front bedroom, Mack right behind her.

Jenna switched on the overhead light and they stood

for a moment, looking up at the ragged hole in the ceiling where Lacey's poor foot had gone through. Jenna made a mental note to call around on Monday, see if she could find someone to fix the thing for her. The drywall would have to be patched and then retextured. She could manage the painting herself.

"Well?" Mack said.

"Just considering the repair bills. Let's look around."

They checked under the bed, in the closet, beneath the bureau and bed tables. Even in the bureau drawers. Nothing.

Mack stood in the middle of the room and looked up at the hole again. "Do you think he could be up there? Maybe Lacey really did hear him."

They decided to give it a shot. Jenna got a flashlight, then they climbed the small, dark set of stairs that went up from the landing. They scoured the cramped, low attic, pushing boxes and old furniture out of the way so they could see behind it, but they found no sign of Byron.

When they got back to the second floor, they went through the rest of the rooms there just in case—the other two bedrooms, the two bathrooms and the big closet on the landing.

When there was nowhere else to look, they trudged back down the stairs and into Jenna's bathroom. Jenna sat on the edge of the tub and rinsed the attic dust from her feet and hands, ending by splashing the clear, warm water on her face. Mack waited until she was finished, then rinsed the dust off himself, as well.

They returned to the bedroom and settled back down in bed. Mack pulled her close.

She laid her head on his chest. He stroked her arm

tenderly and she listened to the strong, steady beating of his heart.

After a while, she whispered a confession. "I don't think I really heard him. I think I only *wanted* to." She felt Mack's lips against her hair and asked, "Do you think we'll ever find him?"

"Hell, Jenna. How would I know?"

She lifted her head, found his eyes through the darkness. "It doesn't matter if you know. Just say yes."

"All right. Yes." With his thumb he wiped away the two tears that had somehow managed to get away from her and trail down her cheeks.

She sniffed and laid her head back down. "I guess I can probably go to sleep now."

He spoke once more, his voice low and infinitely soft. "I love you, Jenna. I've always loved you."

"I know, Mack. I love you, too."

"Love wasn't enough before, was it?"

"No, Mack. It wasn't."

"Will it be enough now?" Something in his voice made her certain that he smiled then, though she still lay against his chest and could not see his face. "Now it's your turn to say yes, whether you really know the answer or not."

She lifted her head again. "Yes." He kissed the end of her nose. Then she asked cautiously, "Are you… ready to talk about it now? About the things each of us wants? About whether we could make our lives fit together again?"

He looked at her deeply. Then he settled her head back onto his chest. "Not now. We have a week and a day left of our original agreement. Let's make the most of it. We can work everything out at the end."

Chapter 14

They brought Lacey home the next day, Sunday. The doctor said it would be several weeks before she could walk without the aid of a crutch.

Mack carried her into the house from the car. She was groggy from the painkillers she'd been given and fell asleep shortly after Mack laid her on the sofa bed. Jenna and Mack tiptoed out, closing both sets of louvered doors, the one to the kitchen and the one to the central hall.

Lacey slept a lot the next couple of days. Jenna checked on her frequently, making sure she was comfortable, that she had everything she needed.

But Lacey had no use for coddling. She kept shooing Jenna away, insisting that she was fine. She knew how to use her crutches if she needed them. She could hobble to the bathroom and the kitchen well enough.

She tried to be upbeat, but Jenna could see the worry

in her eyes. She'd planned to take a few weeks off, and then go back to Southern California and find herself another job. A few weeks now looked as if it might stretch into a few months. She'd had to call her L.A. roommate and tell her she'd better find someone else to help with the rent.

Also, Lacey had let her health insurance lapse after she'd lost her most recent waitress job. To pay for her surgery she'd had to dip into the money their mother had left her. Jenna offered to help out, but Lacey only shook her head and said she could and would pay her own bills.

Jenna tried not to worry about her. But the cheerful facade was such a very thin veneer. Lacey's blue eyes had circles under them. And she didn't put much effort into personal hygiene. Her gorgeous golden hair hung lank around her shoulders.

Twice, Jenna tried to bring up the subject of Logan. Both times, Lacey shook her head. "Let it be, Jenna," she said. "Just…leave it alone."

"If you ever want to talk about it, you know I'm here."

"Thanks, but there's nothing to talk about."

So Jenna left it alone. She fussed over her sister as much as Lacey would allow. And she checked on the shop daily, but let her clerks keep the schedules she had set for them during the time she was supposed to have been away. She had the ceiling of the upstairs room repaired and retextured and even bought the paint she needed to finish the job.

Mack had business of his own to tend to. He went out Monday and returned with a carful of computer equipment. He set it all up in one of the spare rooms on the second floor. He spent a few hours a day in there, on the internet, presumably trading stocks.

The majority of the time, though, Jenna and Mack managed to be together. They devoted a portion of that time to hunting for Byron.

Jenna called the local animal shelter and reported the cat missing. The woman at the shelter assured her that since the cat wore an identifying tag on his collar, Jenna would be notified immediately should the cat be brought in.

They had flyers made, with a picture of Byron, Jenna's name, address and phone number, the number on Byron's tag, and an offer of a reward. They tacked the flyers up all over the neighborhood, and even went around knocking on doors, asking people if they'd seen a short-haired black cat with some gray around the neck and a blue studded collar. No one had.

After they'd put up the flyers and talked to the neighbors, they told each other that Byron would show up sometime soon.

And they focused on enjoying themselves, on making the most of every moment they had. They drove down to Sacramento for a couple of evenings out, where they ate at good restaurants, went to a play one night and a movie the other. Then they rode back up to the foothills after midnight to enjoy what was left of the darkness in Jenna's bed.

Closer to home, they explored the local tourist attractions, climbing down into the cool, moist caves of hardrock gold mines together, wandering the rooms of a couple of gingerbread-decked historic Victorian houses. On Wednesday they took a long drive up into the mountains, where the fall colors were already in full show.

They kept to the agreement they'd made to work everything out when the two weeks were over. Sometimes Jenna wondered at their mutual reticence when it came to discussing the future. But she didn't allow herself to wonder too long or too deeply. This lovely time they shared was finite. She didn't want to waste a minute of it stewing over the differences that could push them apart.

On Thursday Lacey asked Jenna if she'd pick up a few art supplies for her, a couple of big sketch pads and some charcoals and pastels. Jenna took this as a good sign that Lacey was ready to do more than read and watch TV and worry about the money she didn't have. Jenna and Mack drove down to Sacramento to the store Lacey had recommended.

On the way, Mack quizzed Jenna. He found out that Lacey painted in oils and in watercolors, as well. He grabbed a clerk the minute they got to the store and drilled the man on what kinds of equipment Lacey might need.

Besides the items Lacey had asked for, Mack ended up buying an easel, a number of blank canvases already stretched across wood frames and a set each of oil and watercolor paints. He also chose a worktable that could be folded up into an easy-to-carry suitcase, as well as several high-quality brushes.

As he strolled the aisles of the art supply store, grabbing things the clerk had suggested and throwing them into the cart, Jenna tried to explain to him that Lacey would probably be upset when she saw all he'd bought. He'd spent so much more than she could afford.

"I'm not letting her pay for it," Mack said. "So don't worry about that."

"But Mack. Her self-esteem right now is at an all-time low. And she has a lot of pride. She'll insist on paying for it."

"So? She can insist all she wants. As far as I'm concerned, she needs to be doing something she loves, something worthwhile. I'm just making sure she has the materials for it."

"But—"

"Save the buts, Jenna. I'm doing this."

When they returned to Meadow Valley and Mack and Jenna began lugging all their purchases into the back parlor, Lacey didn't say a word. At first. She sat in the easy chair, watching them troop in and out, her lips a thin line and her arms crossed under her breasts.

"Is that all of it?" she asked at last with pained civility.

"You bet." Mack set the folded easel against the fireplace. He was grinning. "I talked to the clerk at that store where you sent us. He told me the kinds of things you might need, so I bought 'em."

"I asked for some sketch pads, and something to draw with. Period."

"Yeah, well. You need all this other stuff if you're going to really get some work done."

"Who said I planned to 'really get some work done'?" She quoted him directly, with a sneer twisting her lips. "You can just pack all this stuff up and take it back where you got it. I didn't ask for it and I don't want it."

Mack wasn't grinning anymore. "Oh. Sorry. I guess

I misunderstood. Your sister told me that you were an *artist*."

Lacey's white skin had flushed a deep red. "I *am* an artist, thank you very much."

"Well, then. If you're an artist, you need all this stuff."

"I cannot afford all this stuff." Lacey cast an outraged glance at Jenna, who was standing near the doors to the hall, wondering if she should say something or just let the two of them duke it out. "Jenna, tell him he has no right to—"

"Leave Jenna out of this," Mack commanded. "She already told me not to buy what you need. I did it anyway. So she's in the clear here."

"She is not. She brought you into this house and—"

He let out a groan. "Oh, come on. Let's get back to the real issue. I can afford all this stuff. Believe me. It's less than nothing to me. And you need it. You need it very badly."

"You have no idea what I need."

"Sure I do. You need to paint. Right? Because you're an artist and that's what you do. And you also have several weeks where you won't be able to do much else. If you look at it that way, this could be the perfect opportunity for you."

Lacey actually rolled her eyes—but the hot color was fading from her cheeks. "'The perfect opportunity.' Oh, brother."

"Think about it," Mack said. "Give it twenty-four hours. I'll just leave all this equipment right where it is until then. If you decide that maybe you can use it, then it stays. Otherwise, Jenna and I will take it all back."

Lacey looked more pensive now than furious. "I suppose it would be pretty inconvenient for you to have to drive all the way back down to the valley just to return everything."

"Yeah," Mack said. "It would."

Jenna hid a smile. The inconvenience would be minimal, and they all knew it. She and Mack had driven down to Sacramento and back three times already. They'd probably go again, for dinner and a show. They could easily cart all the art supplies along with them.

But she had a feeling that wouldn't be necessary. She had a feeling Lacey was going to give in and let Mack provide what she needed.

And she felt such pride—pride and the tender sweetness of her love. Yes, pride and love. The two emotions mingled together, making her chest tight and her eyes a little bit misty.

She wondered if Mack even knew how much he had changed in the past seven years. The old Mack would never have done such a thing for her sister—not from any smallness of spirit, but because it never would have occurred to him.

The old Mack had no time for other people's needs. He'd been too busy trying to fill the bottomless need inside himself.

Mack added, "I mean it. We'll take it all back tomorrow. That is, if you decide you're not going to use it…"

The next morning, when Jenna and Mack were tiptoeing around the kitchen trying to get themselves some breakfast without waking the night owl, Lacey called to them from the other side of the louvered doors.

"You can stop whispering and giggling in there. I'm awake."

Mack called back, "Real men don't giggle."

"Sorry. Whispering and laughing, then."

"That's better. Want coffee?"

"Yes. Black."

Jenna carried it in to her.

Lacey was sitting up against the backrest of the sofa bed and smiling sleepily. "Thanks. I can use that." Jenna handed over the hot drink and Lacey sipped. "Mmm." She wrapped both hands around the mug. "I had an idea...."

Jenna slipped off her shoes and sat down on the bed, scooting up against the backrest so that she and her sister sat shoulder-to-shoulder. "Tell me."

"You know those old floor screens up in the attic, the ones with the teak frames and the rice paper botanical prints down the center of each panel?"

"What about them?"

Lacey sipped more coffee. "Do you think you and Mack could bring them down here for me?"

"What are you planning to do with those old things?"

Lacey glanced at the northeast corner of the room, where sunlight streamed in the double-hung window next to the fireplace. "The light's not too bad in that corner. I want to set up a sort of studio over there. Put up that easel Mack bought me and get a couple of straight chairs, one for me to sit on, one for my foot. I'll use the screens to divide off the space." Lacey fiddled with the hem of the melon-colored T-shirt she'd worn to sleep in, the T-shirt Jenna had brought her from Seal Beach. "You know how I am when I'm working on something. I don't like anyone peeking over my shoulder."

Jenna laid her hand on her sister's. "We'll get those screens down here right after breakfast."

Lacey set the mug on the little table to the left of the bed and leaned her head on Jenna's shoulder. "Mack's right. I have all this time. I should put it to good use."

"Yes. That was good advice."

"He's changed," Lacey said softly. "When he was here all those years ago, I don't think he said more than two words to me. Hello. Goodbye. That was it. He wasn't…interested in some messed-up kid with a chip on her shoulder, even if that kid was your little sister. But now, well, he's just not the same SOB I remember so fondly."

Jenna chuckled. "Yes. He *has* changed."

Lacey lifted her head. "So. Will you get married— or stay married…or whatever?"

"I don't know yet."

"When *will* you know?"

"Sunday or Monday. We're going to talk it all over then. And until then, we're just going to be together and love every minute of it."

"People should do that more often—just be together and love every minute of it." Lacey looked away. Then she sighed and rested her head on Jenna's shoulder again. "You smell good." She pulled back, lifted a lock of her own limp hair off her shoulder and looked at it critically. "Haven't washed this in a couple of days, have I?"

"Has it really been that long?" Jenna made her voice light.

Lacey pulled a face. "You are disgustingly tactful."

"Was that a compliment?"

"Yeah. I guess it was."

After breakfast, Lacey disappeared into the bathroom under the stairs. When she came out, she smelled of bath powder and her hair had regained its old luster. Meanwhile Jenna and Mack brought down the screens. They dusted them off and set them up to divide off the area Lacey would use as her studio.

Once the screens were in place, Lacey told them where to put the chairs she needed as well as her new worktable, the easel, the various supplies and the stack of blank canvases. Then she told them to get lost.

"And no peeking behind these screens." She spoke to both of them, but she was looking at Mack. She knew that Jenna already understood how she felt about privacy when she worked. "I want to feel confident that no one will see what I'm doing until I'm ready to let them see."

Mack grunted. "What do you want, an oath signed in blood?"

Lacey let out a groan. "Go on, get out of here, both of you. Give me some peace and quiet."

Jenna and Mack were only too happy to oblige.

Friday went by way too fast. Lacey sat in the easy chair and sketched—and then disappeared behind her screens for hours at a time. Mack and Jenna painted the ceiling of the room upstairs. By the time they were finished, Jenna said it was impossible to tell there had ever been a hole in it.

Saturday dawned warm and bright. It almost might have been summer again, the day was so mild.

Jenna packed a picnic lunch. She and Mack put on jeans and sturdy shoes and drove up into the mountains again. They found a side road and followed it until the pavement gave out and the ruts got too deep to make it safe to go on. Then they took their lunch and a big old blue-and-red quilt and they started walking through the tall pines. The trail they chose wound up the side of a hill.

They found what they sought when they crested the hill: a small glen, with a grassy plot of ground, trees all around and a stream bubbling cheerfully over a rocky outcropping a few feet away.

They spread their blanket and ate their lunch. Jenna had packed sugar cookies for dessert.

"You've got sugar on your mouth," Mack said when she had finished her cookie and brushed the crumbs from her hands.

She gave him a teasing smile, one that had him scooting close and guiding her down onto the blanket.

He kissed her, running his tongue over her lips first, licking the sugar away.

He chuckled. "Sweetest kiss I ever had."

She lay looking up at him, into those eyes that were like a cloudy sky. Overhead, the pine branches moved and sighed together in the warm autumn wind.

He kissed her again and she closed her eyes. She felt as if she floated, so much like the way it had been in her dream of him. The two of them, floating in this little glen on the faded blue-and-red squares of the quilt.

If only they could float like this forever....

After a time, he pulled back. He put his hand on the side of her face. His skin was warm, slightly rough. She turned her head, pressed her lips against his palm.

"One more day," he whispered.

She sighed, and the sound seemed to come not only from inside her, but from the wind in the trees, from all around. "Yes. Just one more…" She touched his face, as he was touching hers, and she wondered why she felt so sad at the thought that their two weeks were almost past.

After all, they knew now that they had love. And for the past few glorious days, love *had* been enough.

And they had both changed over the years. They'd changed in positive ways. Surely they could make it work now.

Mack kissed her some more. She lifted her arms and wrapped them around him. He sank down upon her, on the blue-and-red quilt, in the private little glen at the crest of the hill with the warm wind sighing around them. She pulled Mack tighter, kissed him harder, to make her silly doubts go away.

Not much later, the wind turned cooler. Clouds began to gather. They straightened their clothing and packed away what was left of the lunch they had shared. Then they rolled up the quilt and started down the hill.

The rain began just as they reached the car—and ended right after they got to the house. They found Lacey's doors closed, which meant she was probably working and didn't want to be disturbed. They retreated to Jenna's bedroom, kicked off their shoes and lay down on the bed to continue what the short storm had interrupted.

Mack kissed her and she kissed him back and wished that tomorrow would never have to come. That this could go on forever, the two of them, spending long, lazy days just being together, talking and laughing and making slow, tender love.

When the doorbell rang, they still had most of their clothes on.

Mack lifted his head. "Who's that?"

"I don't know. Maybe Lacey's expecting someone."

Jenna sat up and reached for her shirt, which Mack had tossed to the foot of the bed. She stuck her arms in the sleeves and began buttoning up. Mack rolled to his back and lay there, watching her in that special way that spread warmth in her belly and made her fingers awkward and slow.

He raised his arms and laced them behind his head. She stared dreamily at his bare chest, at the powerful muscles of his flexed arms.

He grinned. "Hurry back."

"You know I will." She managed to button that last button, then tucked the shirt into the waistband of her jeans. She bent close to give him one more kiss before she rose and padded on bare feet to the front door.

The visitor was a boy. A boy she'd never seen before.

He looked about ten and he carried a battered skateboard tucked under one scrawny arm. He wore a grimy baseball cap turned sideways and pants five sizes too big, chopped off at the knees. His dingy white T-shirt, also way too big for him, had a rip at the shoulder and the name of some rock-and-roll band emblazoned on the front. His sockless feet were stuck into a pair of unlaced and totally disreputable black sneakers.

Jenna glanced past him, out to the street. No one else waited there. The boy appeared to be alone.

"Yes?" she asked cautiously.

He was clutching a sheet of paper in his free hand. He held it up and Jenna saw that it was one of the flyers she and Mack had plastered all over the neighborhood.

The boy said, "It says here that there's a reward for this cat."

Chapter 15

Hope made Jenna's heart beat faster. "You have my cat?"

"First I wanna know. How much is the reward?"

"But do you have him?"

"Maybe."

Jenna sucked in a calming breath and told her heart to slow down. She didn't know this boy. He hardly looked reliable. "Either you have him, or you don't. Which is it?"

"It depends." The boy was folding up the flyer. "How much is the reward?"

"What's going on?" It was Mack. He'd pulled his shirt on, but his feet, like Jenna's, were still bare. "You have the cat?" He pinned the boy with an accusing glare.

The boy slid the flyer into a pocket and started backing up.

Jenna said, "Wait. We just want to know—"

But the sight of Mack had spooked him. The boy whirled and raced down the walk.

"Stop him!" Jenna cried. "He's got Byron!"

Mack didn't hesitate. He sprinted around her and down the front steps. Jenna took off right behind him. The boy had already leaped the low front gate.

Mack jumped the fence just as the boy was scrambling onto his skateboard. Before the boy could roll out of reach, Mack managed to catch hold of his too-big T-shirt. He gave a hard tug and the boy lost his footing. The skateboard went flying and the boy dropped backward, right into Mack's arms.

"Hey, leggo! Lemme go!" The skateboard shot away down the steep sidewalk. "You better lemme go right now!"

Mack tucked the boy under his arm and started to turn for the gate as the skateboard veered off into the grass several houses away.

"My skateboard!" the boy shouted, flailing wildly with his skinny arms and legs. "Leggo. I've gotta get my skateboard!"

By then, Jenna had begun to reconsider the wisdom of sending Mack after the child. "Mack. Maybe you'd better let him go. I don't think—"

"Help!" The boy shouted. "Kidnappers! Rapers! Somebody help!"

Jenna winced. "Mack. I think you'd better—"

"They've got me! They're killin' me!"

Mack muttered a curse. But he did lower the boy to the ground. The second his feet touched the sidewalk, the kid took off.

Mack called after him. "About the reward? It's ten thousand dollars!"

Jenna gasped. It was a lot of money. Even for a cat as wonderful as Byron.

The dirty tennis shoes skidded to a stop. Slowly the boy turned.

"The reward," Mack said again. "For the cat. Ten thousand dollars."

The boy stared for a full count of five. Then he turned again and trotted down to where his skateboard had veered off the sidewalk.

Once he had the skateboard tucked safely under his arm, he faced Mack once more. "Nobody pays that much money for an old black cat."

"I do," Mack said.

"Why?"

"Because I can afford it. And I want the cat back."

"You rich?"

"Yeah. I'm rich."

The boy looked down at his dirty sneakers, then back up at Mack. "Listen. I didn't *steal* him or anything. He just showed up. He wanted to hang around. Okay, yeah, I fed him. But I didn't feed him much. He stayed anyway. It's not like he's a *prisoner*. He could go any time he wanted to."

"Ten thousand," Mack said again. "Where is the cat?"

The boy took off his hat, looked into it, and then plunked it back on his head. "This better be for real."

"It's for real," Mack said. "But tell me. Is this cat a talker? Meows all the time?"

The kid looked down again, shifted his skateboard from one hand to the other, and shook his head. "Naw.

He does nothin' but purr all the time. He purrs real loud." The boy reached into his back pocket and pulled out the folded flyer. "But he's got on a blue collar and a tag with the number you gave on this paper."

Mack looked at Jenna then. "Sounds like Bub to me."

She nodded and drew in a deep breath to slow her racing pulse. Joy was shimmering through her. Byron was all right.

Mack turned to the boy again. "What's your name?"

The boy said nothing, only glared in defiance as he stuffed the flyer back into his pocket.

"Come on. Your name."

The boy gave in and muttered, "Riley."

"Okay, Riley. You get ten thousand dollars if you give us back the cat."

Riley considered, trying hard to look unimpressed, though excitement made his black eyes shine. At last, he nodded. "Okay. Deal."

Mack gestured at Jenna. "This is Jenna. I'm Mack. Why don't you come inside while we put our shoes on?"

Riley's mouth twisted with disdain. "Fuggetaboutit. I don't go inside a stranger's house. I'll wait on the porch."

"Fair enough."

Jenna saved her second thoughts until she and Mack were alone in her bedroom, yanking on their shoes and tying up the laces. "You're not really going to give ten thousand dollars to that boy, are you? He can't be more than ten or eleven years old."

"What? You want me to cheat him?"

"Of course not. But that's a lot of money to just hand to a child."

He finished tying his second shoe. "I assume he's

got parents, or someone who looks after him. We can give the money to them—and hurry up. Who knows how long that kid will wait out there?"

Jenna grabbed her purse and Mack grabbed his keys, wallet and checkbook and they hurried out the door.

Riley refused to get into the Lexus. "Get in a stranger's car? You think I'm outta my mind? You follow me, I'll lead you there. I can move pretty fast on my skateboard."

He wasn't exaggerating. He flew down West Broad Street, his stringy hair blowing out from under his cap, and turned the corner at Hill Street so swiftly and sharply that Jenna couldn't hold back a gasp.

He kept going, never breaking stride, down steep streets and around tight corners. Mack and Jenna, in the Lexus, did manage to keep up, but came close to losing sight of him more than once when he suddenly spun around a corner and zipped off in another direction.

They ended up on the outskirts of town where small, run-down houses were tucked among the trees. Battered old cars stood on blocks in dirt driveways. And broken toys littered overgrown yards, yards surrounded by rusting chain-link fences.

Riley turned into one of the narrowest driveways, where an aged Day-Glo-green hatchback with a bashed-in driver's door huddled under a listing carport. Mack pulled in behind the green car. Riley was already at the side door of the dilapidated clapboard house, skateboard under his arm, holding open the sagging screen.

Mack and Jenna got out of the car and went to join him.

"You have to be quiet," Riley said. "If the baby's sleeping, my mom won't like you waking her up."

A long wail from the house put an end to that concern.

Riley winced. "Never mind. She's awake."

The boy led them into a small, dingy kitchen, where ancient linoleum, worn through to black in spots, covered the floor, and a yowling baby sat in a high chair, pounding tiny angry fists on the tray. A thin woman with lank dark hair was trying to feed the baby some kind of cereal, but the child kept yowling and spitting out the food.

The woman turned when they entered, her dark eyes first widening in surprise, then quickly narrowing down to slits. "Riley. What's this?"

"They're here for Blackie, Mom," the boy announced. "And they're paying a big reward."

The baby continued to scream.

The woman's eyes narrowed farther. "What reward?"

"Money, Mom. Lots of it." The boy raised his voice to compete with the screams of the baby and the drone of the television that reached them from the open doorway to the next room. He pulled the flyer from the back pocket of his ragged pants and held it out. His mother took it and peered at it doubtfully.

"Ten thousand dollars," Riley said with unmistakable pride. "They're gonna pay us ten thousand dollars for that cat, Mom."

The woman's mouth dropped open. Then she shut it tight. She wadded up the flyer and tossed it on the table.

Shaking her head, she stood, went to the sink, grabbed a soggy washcloth and returned to gently wipe the screaming baby's mouth. That accomplished, she dropped the washcloth next to the flyer and pulled the baby from the chair. She laid the child over her shoulder and patted her on the back.

"There, there, Lissa, don't you cry. It's okay. It's okay, now…."

The baby let out one more long wail—and then quieted, hiccuping a few times and grabbing on to the woman with tiny pink hands. "Better?" asked the woman tenderly. "You feel better now?"

The baby hiccuped again and the woman patted her back some more, sending a scathing glance first at Mack, then at Jenna. "What is this? Ten thousand dollars for an old stray cat? Who you think you're trying to fool?"

"We're not fooling anyone." Mack's deep voice was flat. "Mrs.…."

"You from Child Welfare, is that it? Some new trick you people are pulling now? Telling crazy lies to an eleven-year-old boy? We are doing the best we can here, mister. We don't need any tricks played on us, you hear?"

Jenna stepped forward then. "Please. I'm Jenna Bravo and this is Mack McGarrity. We are not from Child Welfare. That black cat means a lot to us. We just want him back."

The baby was starting to fuss again. The woman rocked from side to side trying to soothe her. "Honey, honey, it's okay…." She scowled straight at Jenna. "That cat's in the other room. You take it and go."

Riley grabbed his mother's arm. "Mom! We can have the money, can't we? They said they'd pay, Mom. We got a right to the money."

The woman shook him off and went on rocking the baby. "Hush, you're scaring Lissa. No one pays that kind of money for a cat. Just give those folks what they came for and let them go."

"But—"

"Riley Kettleman, I don't want to have to tell you again."

Riley stared at his mother, mutiny in his eyes. But she looked straight back at him over the downy head of the baby girl. The boy was the one who looked away first. His thin shoulders slumped.

He turned to Mack and Jenna. "Come on. He's in here."

Riley led them into a cramped living room where two other children, a boy and a girl, were sprawled on the threadbare brown carpet, watching cartoons. Byron lay between them. The cat looked up at them and yawned.

Jenna's heart lifted. "Oh. Glad to see us, are you?"

As usual, Byron said nothing.

Riley scooped him up and scratched him behind the ear. "Gonna miss you, Blackie." He handed the cat to Jenna. Byron was purring quite loudly by then. Jenna grinned at the familiar sound.

The girl on the floor, who was probably about six, blinked and tore her gaze away from the images on the television screen. "Hey. They're takin' Blackie?"

"He's theirs," Riley said. "They got the right."

"I love Blackie!" The little girl's eyes filled with tears.

"Don't be a jerk, Tina," Riley instructed. "It's their cat and they're takin' him."

Tina sniffed. "I'm not a jerk. I just don't want Blackie to go away."

"Maybe we'll get another cat," Riley bargained, "like a kitten, or something."

"Did Mom say?"

"I'll talk to her. But right now, just say bye to Blackie."

The little girl stood and buried her face in Byron's sleek coat. Then she turned soulful eyes up to Jenna. "Maybe we could come visit him sometimes?"

Riley didn't give Jenna a chance to answer. "He's their cat, Tina. Mom says we have to turn him over and let them go."

Tina poked at the other boy with her bare foot. "Blackie's leaving."

The boy waved a hand, but kept his eyes glued to the TV screen. "Bye...."

Jenna raised Byron to her shoulder. His steady purr droned in her ear as Riley led them back through the kitchen where the baby sat in the high chair again, quiet and contented now as her mother spooned cereal into her mouth. The woman didn't spare them so much as a glance as they went by.

Jenna paused at the door, letting Riley and Mack go out ahead of her. "Mrs. Kettleman?"

The woman granted her a cool look.

"I really appreciate your taking care of my cat."

The woman straightened her shoulders. Her eyes had changed from cold to accusing. "You shouldn't have lied, shouldn't have gotten my boy's hopes up like that. That's maybe the worst thing in the world, hope. It lifts you up and then you end up crashing down."

"It wasn't a lie. Mack is willing to pay the money he offered."

The woman blew out a disgusted breath, then turned back to her baby. She dipped up a spoon of cereal and patiently poked it into Lissa's tiny pink mouth.

Jenna hesitated, thinking she ought to say more.

But what? Riley Kettleman's mother had clearly heard enough. She pulled open the door and left the kitchen.

Outside, Mack was leaning against the Lexus, writing a check.

Riley stood a few feet away, his head tipped to the side, watching Mack warily. "My mom said not to take your—"

Mack looked straight into Riley's dark eyes. "Do you want the money or not?"

Riley chewed his lower lip. "I thought it would be cash money. Checks bounce. I know that."

"This one won't."

"Yeah. Right."

"Listen. This check is drawn on a national bank. There's a branch of that bank right here in Meadow Valley. You get your mother to take this check to that branch. They'll cash it for her."

Riley gulped. And then he nodded.

Mack asked, "You think you can get her to take it in and cash it?"

Riley bit his lower lip, considering, then nodded again. "I'll say, what have we got to lose? Either things will still be the same as they are now, or we'll have ten thousand dollars we didn't have before."

"Good thinking." Mack bent to the checkbook again. "Her last name is Kettleman, right?"

"Yeah."

"How do you spell it?"

Slowly Riley spelled the name.

"I need her first name, too."

"Erin. *E-R-I-N.*"

Mack glanced up. "Or maybe I should make it out to your father?"

Riley lifted his head high. "Like that'll do anybody any good. My dad is dead."

Byron purred all the way home. The sound filled up the quiet car. Jenna petted her cat and felt so grateful to have him back—grateful and sad at the same time.

Sad for Erin Kettleman and her four children. Sad for Erin's husband, who had died and left a struggling family behind. She closed her eyes and said a little prayer that Riley's mother wouldn't tear up Mack's check. That she'd take a chance on hope one more time.

Jenna glanced over at Mack. He was staring straight ahead and didn't see the tender smile she gave him.

She almost spoke, but what was there to say? Some comfortable platitude? Some cliché? *That poor woman...those poor children...?*

No. Better just to ride in silence, with Byron purring on her lap and Mack in the driver's seat, taking them home.

Lacey was almost as happy as Jenna to have Byron home again. She hugged him and he allowed her to fuss over him, purring contentedly for her as he did for everyone else.

She scolded him. "Oh, I just felt so terrible, you naughty boy. And here you are, look at you, back home again and none the worse for wear." She beamed up at Jenna. "He looks great."

"He sure does."

Lacey gazed down at the cat again and pretended to scowl. "Don't you ever do that again, you bad boy."

Byron looked up at her, yawned and went on purring.

"We should celebrate," Lacey said.

"Absolutely," Jenna agreed, pleased to see the happy color in her sister's cheeks.

Mack spoke up then. "I'll go out and get some steaks and a couple of bottles of wine."

Jenna volunteered, "I'll come with you."

"No. Stay here with your sister. I won't be long."

Something in his tone bothered her. Something distant, something withdrawn.

"Mack? Are you sure you don't want me to—?"

But he was already on his way down the hall.

Jenna shrugged and let him go. She and Lacey fussed over Byron some more and Jenna told Lacey about the small house on the outskirts of town where Riley Kettleman lived.

Lacey said what Jenna kept thinking. "I just hope that woman takes a chance and cashes that check."

When Mack returned, they opened the wine. They proposed several toasts: to Byron, to Riley, to the mysteries of fate. Later, Jenna stuck three potatoes in the oven to bake and tossed a big green salad. Mack grilled the steaks to medium rare perfection on the old gas grill out in the backyard.

They ate in the dining room using the good china.

More than once during the evening, Jenna noticed that Mack seemed preoccupied. But the minute she'd catch his eye or ask him a question, his distant expression would vanish. He would smile and answer her warmly. She'd tell herself that she was just imagining that faraway look in his eyes.

Later, when Jenna and Mack retired to her room, they made slow, perfect love, which neither inclement weather nor a knock at the door interrupted. Jenna thought it was the best kind of ending to a very special day. She fell asleep smiling, with Mack's arms around her and Byron purring steadily from the foot of the bed.

Her dreams, however, were disturbing ones.

In one, Riley Kettleman flew down a busy street on his skateboard, sliding in and around large, threatening vehicles. The drivers honked at him and slammed on their brakes. Some of the drivers even leaned out their windows and shook their fists and swore. Riley ignored them. He rolled on down the street, fearless and fleet as the wind.

The street faded away. And Riley's mother stood in her small, run-down kitchen and tore up Mack's check. The walls of the rickety house fell in and the pieces of the check blew away in the autumn wind.

And then Jenna and Mack drifted by on the white bed. Mist curled around them. They were in that floating, hazy void again. But now they weren't making love. They were just…sitting there, looking at each other. Jenna reached out her hand to him. But some invisible barrier stood between them. She couldn't touch him.

She called to him, her cries getting louder and more frantic as she saw that he didn't hear her. He only sat there, looking at her so sadly, a few inches…and a thousand miles away.

She began to cry.

The tears were trailing down her face, into her hair, as she opened her eyes.

She was lying on her back, staring at the ceiling. It was still dark.

Jenna sniffed and swiped at her cheeks, turning to her side where she could see the bedside clock.

"Jenna?" The sound of his voice, so tender and deep.

Her heart twisted. He touched her shoulder. She rolled to her back again and he canted up on an elbow to look down at her. His eyes gleamed at her through the shadows.

"Our last day," she said.

He saw her tears, gently rubbed them away. "Not yet. It's still night."

"It's 3:00 a.m. Technically, it's tomorrow."

White teeth flashed as he smiled. "Just like technically, we're still married."

"Yes, Mack. We are. And we have to talk."

"We will."

"When?"

"After breakfast. Will that do?"

"Okay." She sighed. "I had bad dreams. I couldn't reach you. You were right there…but I couldn't touch you. And that boy, Riley—"

"Shh." He turned her on her side again, pulled her in against him, so that they lay spoon fashion, his body cradling hers.

"Do you think they'll be all right? That boy. His mother…the other three children?"

He smoothed her hair away from her cheek and brushed a kiss against her ear. "Go to sleep, Jenna. Just go to sleep."

"Oh, Mack. Why is the world so cruel?"

He kissed her again. But he didn't answer.

"Mack? Whatever happens, I want you to know that this has been the best two weeks of my life."

He chuckled then. "Right. We went to a funeral in Long Beach. Bub ran away and your sister broke her foot."

"We met Alec and Lois. And my sister is going to

be okay, and Byron is home again now. And I think we did something really important. I think we…found out why we got married in the first place. We found out that there *was* love between us, that it never really died. Now, no matter what, when I think of you, I'll think of the good things."

"So," he whispered softly. "No regrets?"

For some reason she chose not to examine, tears filled her eyes again. She blinked them way. "Absolutely none."

"Good. Now go back to sleep."

He pulled her closer. Byron tiptoed from the foot of the bed to stretch out beside them.

It wasn't long at all before sleep came to claim her again.

Chapter 16

They woke together with the dawn. In the kitchen they moved about quietly, brewing coffee, poaching eggs, buttering toast. Lacey didn't call to them from behind the louvered doors, so it was just the two of them at the table with Byron sitting on the little rag rug in the corner, purring and giving himself a thorough morning bath.

"Let's get out of the house," Jenna said once they'd scraped the plates and put them in the dishwasher. "Away from the possibility that the phone will ring or someone will knock on the door."

"All right."

Outside, the air was brisk and the wind had a bite to it. Mack wore his leather jacket and Jenna had pulled on her old red plaid mackinaw coat. They got in the Lexus.

Mack asked, "Where to?"

"How about where we had our picnic yesterday? I don't think anyone will bother us there."

Mack parked the car in the same place that they'd left it the day before. They got out and he went around to the trunk for the blue-and-red quilt.

He tossed the quilt over his shoulder. "Let's go."

They started into the trees.

It was much cooler in the little glen at the crest of the hill than it had been the day before. But since they both had their jackets, it was bearable. They spread the quilt and Jenna found four smooth rocks to hold the corners down. Then she sat, tucking her legs to the side and shivering a little as the chilly wind found its way under the warm wool of her mackinaw.

Mack stood above her, at the edge of the blanket, his hands in his pockets.

She looked up at him and forced a smile, though she felt terribly nervous all of a sudden. "Sit with me." She patted the blanket beside her.

He let her suggestion pass without response. He was looking at her mouth. "Your lip is twitching."

She pressed both lips together in an effort to make the twitching stop. It didn't help. "I know."

"I don't…know where to start."

Neither did she, really. She pulled at a loose thread on the quilt and tried to organize her thoughts, which suddenly seemed to be spinning off in a thousand different directions at once.

"We could start at the beginning," he said.

She nodded. "That sounds right."

Mack dropped to a crouch, picked up a twig from the yellowing grass and broke it in two. "When you called me and told me you were going to marry the doctor, at first I was stunned. Just at the idea that you could even think of marrying someone else…" He paused then, to toss both bits of twig away, one and then the other. "It seemed impossible to me." He laughed, a dry sound. "That's my ego for you. Here we'd been apart for seven years, should have been divorced for five. I hadn't seen you in all that time. And yet…" He sat then, on the edge of the blanket, and wrapped his arms around his knees. "I couldn't just let it go. I had to see you again, had to try…" He seemed not to know how to go on. He looked up at the pine branches swaying overhead, then down at the blanket, then across the glen, where the clear water of the little stream burbled cheerfully over the rocks.

Finally he tried again. "What I'm saying is, I didn't really think it through all that well. I just knew I had to get myself some time with you, one way or another, to find out if maybe you felt the same as I did, to see if there was still anything there for you, when you thought about me."

The wind blew Jenna's hair against her mouth. She brushed it away. "And so now you know. There's still something there."

"Yes. Now I know."

"And the question is…what do we do about it?"

He nodded.

She wanted to touch him, wanted to reach out and put her hand against his cheek. She wanted to feel his lips against her palm. And then she wanted his mouth touching her own, his body covering hers, shielding her against the chill of the wind.

When they touched, it always seemed as if there was no need for words. When they touched, she could forget the future, and put aside the past. When they touched, there was only the moment, only right now.

But they couldn't put off discussing the future forever. The time *had* come to deal with what would happen next.

She kept her hands to herself. "I love Meadow Valley, Mack. You know I do. But I don't...I don't *need* to live here the way I did once. I don't feel that a place defines who I am anymore. I realize now that I could have done better, when we lived in New York. I could have tried harder to make a new life there."

He scanned her face, his gaze intent. "You're saying you'd move to Florida with me now?"

"I would. Yes. I'd give it a try. And a *real* try this time. We could fix up that house of yours—you did say it needs fixing up?"

"Yes, I did."

"And you could teach me to fish. Isn't that what you do on that boat of yours—fish?"

"Yeah. I fish. And sometimes I just drift."

"I could do that. Drift. Up to a point."

He shifted, looked away again. "Up to what point?"

And she said, as clearly and firmly as her suddenly tight throat would allow, "I want children, Mack. I always have. I think you know that. I want...an ordinary, everyday, garden-variety family. I want a husband who's around a reasonable amount of time."

He turned to face her again. "A husband who's around. That, I can do now. I can be there, with you, whenever you need me."

"Yes. I know. And it's..." She swallowed, took a breath, and said, "It's almost enough."

"Almost?"

"Yes. Oh, Mack…" There it was again. That overpowering urge to reach out. But she didn't do it. She laced her hands together in her lap and chose her words with utmost care. "I want kids we can love and raise together. Our own babies, if that's possible. But if for some reason we couldn't have children, then I'd want to adopt. I just want to do that, to help some little ones grow up and start their own life. To me, that's the most important thing there is. I wouldn't feel I'd really lived if I didn't raise a child or two."

He said nothing. His eyes were tender and sad.

"Would you…do that with me, have a family with me, Mack? Do you think that you could?"

He spoke then, but only to say her name soft and low. "Jenna…"

She bit her lip to keep from begging him. All those years ago she had begged him. It had done no good.

She doubted that it would do much good now.

Her nose was starting to run. And a few pointless tears had gotten away from her. She felt in the pocket of her mackinaw and found a tissue. Carefully she smoothed it out. Then she blew her nose and wiped the tears from her cheeks.

Mack rose to his full height as she slid the soggy tissue back into her pocket. He walked a few feet away and stood staring down the trail they had climbed up the side of the hill.

She thought he looked so tall and strong standing there—tall and strong and utterly alone. She ached for him, for the lost little boy he had been long ago, for the driven young man who couldn't slow down enough to be a husband to her—and for the drifting, footloose millionaire he was now, the man who still hadn't found real meaning in his life.

Finally he turned to her again. He came back to the blanket, but stopped at the edge. "I keep thinking about that kid, Jenna. About Riley Kettleman. About that baby, little Lissa—and those two other kids, Tina and whatever the other boy's name was. I keep thinking that those kids haven't got a prayer. That their father is gone and their mother can't provide for them. That it's the same old story, over and over. People start out with the best damn intentions. They get together and they have children. And then something happens. Divorce. Death. Lost jobs, lost hopes…" His voice had gone rough, as if something inside him were tearing. He paused, stuck his hands into his jacket pockets, pulled them out again. "Jenna, I just don't think I can do that. Bring some kid into the world, into my life. Kids… they don't understand. They trust. They believe that you will take care of them. But that doesn't always happen. Things go wrong, things you can never anticipate. And children are left with less than nothing. I couldn't do that to another human being."

She really hadn't meant to touch him. But she couldn't stop herself. She reached up, took his hand. "Mack…"

He didn't pull away, but he didn't come down to her, either. He only looked at her through bleak and lonely eyes. "I know," he said. "It's not rational, that I feel that way. You're not Erin Kettleman. You've got a business, you own a house. You're a woman with your own resources.

"And I've got money now. I could protect the ones I loved, no matter what happened to me. I could see to it that you never ended up like Riley's mother, living in a run-down shack with four children and no way out, or like my own mother, feeling you had to make a choice between your children and a man." His fingers tightened over hers, hard enough that her bones ground together. But she did not wince, and she didn't pull away.

"In my mind, I understand," he said. "In my mind, I realize that the chances my children will end up like I did are minimal, that even if we both got hit by a truck, they could still be provided for. But then I think of what it was like for me. To have a family, and then to have nothing. My father dead. My mother just…gone. And my gut knots up and I can't get air. I've even lied to myself that someday I'm going to change, someday I'll let go of all this irrational, faulty reasoning. I'll realize that I'm like just about everyone else. I'll want children.

"But Jenna. It hasn't happened. And the truth is, I don't think it's ever going to happen." He tugged on her hand. "Come up here. Come on."

She let him pull her to her feet.

He wrapped his arms around her, but held himself away enough that he could meet her eyes. "I'm sorry, Jenna. I don't know what the hell I was thinking, to force you into this two weeks with me, when I knew how you felt about having a family—and I also knew that on that issue I hadn't really changed. I'm just a selfish SOB to the end, I guess, and I—"

"Shh." She wrapped her hand around the back of his neck and pulled his head down close to her. With a low sound he buried his face in her hair. The cold wind blew around them. The pine branches swayed and rubbed together, making a sound like a long, drawn-out moan.

"I told you last night," she whispered. "I have no regrets."

And she didn't. Not a one.

Except perhaps regret that she was losing him. Losing him all over again...

Oh, Lord. She couldn't bear it. She *wouldn't* bear it.

Yes, she did long for children. But she didn't want to have them with anyone but Mack. She had learned that the hard way, and she'd hurt her dear friend Logan deeply in the process.

She pulled back enough to swipe the stubborn tears away with her hand. "Mack. Listen. If you feel that you just can't—"

He took her by the shoulders, his fingers digging in. "Don't say it."

She didn't understand. "What?"

"Don't give away your children for me."

"What children? I don't have any children."

"But you will. And you should. You'll make a hell of a mother."

"No. Not without you."

He cupped her face. His palms were warm. "It's not going to work with us, Jenna."

"Don't say that. That's not so. It will work. We'll make it work. This time, we are not going to throw what we have away. Oh, Mack. Please. Just stay here with me in Meadow Valley for a few more weeks. Let me get my sister on her feet again, and put my shop up for sale. Then I'll go with you to Florida. We'll make a life together. A good life. Just say that you'll stay married to me, that you want me as your wife."

Instead of answering, he kissed her, his mouth covering hers with a yearning so powerful, it stole her breath away. She kissed him back, pressing close, warmed by his body against the coldness of the wind, tasting the salt of her own tears on his lips.

We will be all right, she thought. *We'll make it. Somehow.*

If he couldn't let himself have children, so be it. She would have no children, either. Half a dream, after all, was better than no dream at all. She would focus on what they *did* have and let what might have been alone.

Mack was the one who ended the kiss.

And her hopes, as well.

He pulled away and stared into her eyes.

He said, "It won't work, Jenna. I'm leaving today."

Nothing she could say would dissuade him.

When they got back to the house, he went straight upstairs to unhook his computer equipment and take it out to the car. Jenna couldn't bear to watch him getting ready to leave her. She glanced at the door to the back parlor: still shut. And it sounded quiet in there. Lacey might still be sleeping—or she could be hard at work.

Of course, she wouldn't mind the interruption once she learned that Mack was going.

But Jenna turned from the louvered doors without knocking. Mack was leaving. There was nothing Lacey could do about it. No reason to drag her into the final goodbyes.

Jenna trudged to the front parlor and sat on the sofa. She stared blindly out the window at the Boston fern hanging from the eaves above the porch rail, thinking rather numbly that it was getting too cold out there for the fern now. She would have to remember to bring it in tonight.

And tomorrow…

Her mind skittered away from tomorrow.

From all the tomorrows.

Without Mack.

In her side vision she noted a flicker of movement: Byron, tail held high, strutting her way from the arch to the dining room. He came and sat at her feet and looked up at her expectantly.

She patted her knees. He jumped and landed lightly on her lap. She stroked him, long strokes, from the top of his head to the end of his tail. He arched his back and purred his pleasure, then walked in a circle and curled up in a ball. She stared out the window and absently petted his silky head.

She heard Mack come down the stairs and go back up twice, heard the front door opening and closing as he carried the equipment out. Then he went to the bedroom to gather up his things in there.

Too soon, he appeared in the doorway to the hall. He had his garment bag slung over his shoulder and he carried a suitcase in either hand.

Jenna set Byron on the floor and stood. "I'll help you carry that stuff out."

"I can manage."

"No, really. I don't mind." She walked toward him on legs that felt numb. All of her felt numb, actually. A puppet on a string, moving at the commands of her mind, which felt distant from the rest of her, far away. Disconnected.

"Lacey's door is closed," he said. "I don't want to bother her. Will you tell her goodbye for me?"

How considerate, she thought. *He's broken my heart, but he won't disturb my sister.*

She said, "All right. I'll tell her."

Byron approached him. Mack set down the suitcases, laid the garment bag over them. "Hey, Bub…" He bent and scooped up the cat. "You stick close to home now, don't go running off again." The cat dipped his head to get under Mack's hand. Mack stroked him a few times, and scratched him behind the ears. "Bye, Bub." He bent and set the cat down.

He handed her the garment bag and he took the two suitcases. She followed him out.

He'd loaded his computer equipment into the back seat of the Lexus. The red-and-blue blanket and yesterday's empty picnic basket were still in the trunk. Mack set down the suitcases and took the garment bag from her, laying it over them as he had in the house. Then he took out the quilt and the basket and passed them to her. She stood there, shivering a little without her coat, her arms full of the things he had handed her, waiting as he loaded up the trunk. She watched him tuck the suitcases in with the box of mementos his mother had left him. He laid the garment bag over everything and closed the trunk lid.

And then there was nothing more for him to do but get in the car and drive away from her.

A barrage of questions rose to her lips.

Where are you going now? You don't have a flight to Florida yet, do you? Won't it take a while to arrange one? Why don't you just stay here until then?

Why don't you stay here with me?

Why don't you stay here…forever?

She held the questions back. She already knew

the answers to most of them, anyway. And the others hardly mattered.

They stood on the curb, facing each other, her bundle of blanket and basket between them—well, much more than that between them, really: the children she longed for.

And the children he could not bring himself to have.

She saw in his eyes that he wanted to kiss her.

She didn't think she could bear that right then, though she knew that later, in the long, lonely time to come, without him, she would yearn for every kiss that they hadn't shared.

But now was not later. Now she could not bear one more kiss. Now one more kiss would be the difference between numb dignity and senseless, tearful pleading.

She needed her dignity.

Right then, it was all she had left.

She clutched the blanket tighter, and the handle of the basket, too, holding them close and high in front of her, a barrier to his touch.

She hitched in a breath. "Goodbye, Mack."

"Goodbye, Jenna."

He walked around to the driver's-side door. She found herself following him, standing there, waiting, as he slid in behind the wheel, shut the door, started up the engine, then rolled his window down.

"File the damn papers right away," he said. "Understand?"

She stared at him, wondering what he meant. And then she remembered. The divorce papers.

"Yes. I will. I understand."

He saluted her with a quick wave of his hand. Then she stepped back and he pulled away from the curb.

She stood there, staring after him, clutching her blanket and her empty picnic basket to her heart, long after the Lexus had turned the corner and disappeared from view.

Chapter 17

Lacey hobbled out of the back parlor and into the kitchen about half an hour after Mack left. Jenna was sitting at the table, her head bent over a sheet of lined paper. She looked up and pasted on a smile.

Lacey saw the pain behind the smile. "What's happened? Are you all right?"

Jenna licked her lips. They felt very dry, for some reason. "Mack's gone. He said to tell you goodbye."

Lacey maneuvered herself the rest of the way to the table, and lowered herself into a chair. She set her crutches on the floor beside her as Jenna pushed another chair her way. Carefully Lacey lifted her injured foot onto the second chair.

"Coffee or something?" Jenna offered. "Breakfast, maybe?"

Lacey waved at the air. "Forget about that right now. Are you serious? Mack just left?"

Jenna swallowed convulsively. Then she coughed. "He didn't *just* leave. He... We..." She had to swallow again before she could finish. "It didn't work out between us. So yes, now he's gone." She bent over the sheet of paper again.

Her sister's hand came down and covered the paper. Jenna sighed and looked up.

"Talk to me," Lacey said.

"Lacey, I—"

"Come on." Lacey's voice was so gentle. She lifted her hand off the paper. "What's this?"

"I...I was making a list. I was thinking that it would help, for the next few days. To know just where I'm going and what I need to do. There's a lot to do, really. I've got to get back to the shop full-time. I have been neglecting it these past few weeks. And this house..." She looked around the bright, old-fashioned kitchen. "This house really could use a good top-to-bottom cleaning."

Lacey made a small, tender noise and held out her arms.

"And then there's the divorce," Jenna said. "Mack gave me the papers. I have to take care of that. Can't have it dragging out forever this time. It's best if I cut it clean."

Lacey just looked at her, arms still outstretched.

Jenna stared back, defiant—and aware of her own foolishness. Was there really anything to be gained by rejecting an offer of comfort and love?

Jenna rose from her chair and went to kneel beside her sister. She rested her head in Lacey's lap and felt Lacey's gentle hand stroking her hair.

"You still love him?" Lacey asked.

"Mmm-hmm."

"And he still loves you?"

"Yes."

"So why did he leave?"

Jenna sighed again. "Can we just…let it go? I don't really want to go into it now."

"You're acting as if it's pretty much final."

"It is." Jenna lifted her head and looked into her sister's eyes. "It's absolutely final. He's gone and he's not coming back."

The small blue box, tied with a white bow, was waiting on her pillow when Jenna went to her room a few minutes later.

She sat on the edge of the bed, picked up the box and turned it over in her hands.

There was a card attached.

Jenna,

I bought this years ago. In New York. Right after I won the lawsuit and I had the money I'd always wanted, but I didn't have you. I went into a certain store on Fifth Avenue, and I saw this and I wanted it for you. I could damn well afford it. So I bought it. And I've kept it. And I've thought that I would probably never give it to you.

But somehow, this seems the right time.

The note ended there. She turned the card over, hungry for some final word of love, of endearment, of sweet tenderness. There was none. Not even his name.

She tugged on the end of the white ribbon. It fell away into her lap. She lifted the lid.

Inside, on a bed of white satin, sat a small, perfect pin in the shape of a cat. A cat made of diamonds. With twin emeralds for eyes.

She lifted the little cat free of the box and went to the mirror above the big bureau. With great care, she pinned it over her heart.

It wasn't the kind of thing that looked right with the T-shirt and khaki skirt she was wearing. But she admired it anyway, turning it slightly, back and forth, so the stones caught the light and winked at her.

Then she took it off and laid it back in the box. She wrapped the box in the white ribbon and tied the ribbon in a bow. After a little pulling and smoothing, it looked just as it had before she had opened it.

She took the card and the blue box and put them in the bottom drawer of the bureau. The drawer also contained the silver rattle her great-aunt Matty Riordan Bravo had sent from Wyoming when Jenna was born. And a garnet ring Jenna had prized as a child. And also the little velvet case that held her wedding band.

Jenna treasured every item in that drawer, though they were all things she wouldn't wear or use again.

Five days later, on Friday at seven in the evening, Erin Kettleman came knocking on Jenna's door. Her hair was neatly combed, held back with two butterfly clips at her temples. She wore a faded brown jacket and carried a small tan purse.

"Is he here?" she asked. "Mr. McGarrity?"

Jenna's heart gave a little lurch at the sound of his name. "No, he left on Sunday. For Florida, I believe."

Erin Kettleman put her hand, palm flat, against her chest. "I've left Riley with the children. He's very responsible. And Lissa's asleep." Her thin lips tipped upward in a wobbly smile. "I don't know how long she'll stay that way, though. I—"

"Mrs. Kettleman, please. Come in." Jenna reached out and took the other woman by the arm.

Erin Kettleman allowed herself to be led inside to the front parlor.

"Have a seat." Jenna offered the Chippendale-style chair near the sofa.

"Thank you." Erin Kettleman took the chair.

Jenna went to the sofa and perched on the end, close to her guest. "Something to drink?"

"Um. No. I really can't stay long."

"Your jacket?"

"I'll just keep it on." The dark eyes scanned the room. "This is a beautiful old house."

"It was my mother's."

"Your mother's." Erin Kettleman folded her hands over the tan purse that lay in her lap. "Well. That's real nice."

The two women stared at each other. Silence yawned, then both began speaking at the same time.

"I don't know how to—"

"Did you cash the—?"

They both stopped, smiled, apologized.

Then Erin Kettleman said, "Yes. I cashed Mr. McGarrity's check. Riley talked me into it. He can be very convincing, that boy." A wistful gleam came into her eyes. "He's a lot like his daddy, to tell you the truth."

Jenna took in a breath, then released it in a rush. "I'm so glad. That you cashed it."

"And *I'm* so grateful. And sorry for how rude I was last Saturday. I didn't believe it. I couldn't let myself believe it. Lately I've had the feeling that one more disappointment would finish me off. My husband, Riley senior, he died just six months ago. We…we never had much, but when Riley was alive, somehow we always got by. Since he's been gone, though, things have just seemed to go from bad to worse. I've been real scared. Scared we just weren't gonna make it. Scared that…" Erin Kettleman decided against finishing that thought. She pressed her mouth tightly closed and looked away.

Jenna leaned closer and brushed a hand against Erin's worn coat sleeve. "But you weren't disappointed this time, were you?"

"No. No, I was not." There was that quavering smile again. "Let me tell you, that was some moment. I was shaking when I signed the back of that check. And then the teller took it, along with my ID, and punched up some numbers on her computer. *Then* she said, 'How would you like that, Mrs. Kettleman? In hundreds?'" Erin Kettleman let out a short, high-pitched laugh. "My heart just stopped, I'm not kidding you. Just stopped dead right there in my chest. I thought there would never be another moment quite like that one. But I was wrong."

Jenna frowned. "Wrong? How so?"

Erin Kettleman unsnapped the clasp on her purse.

She reached in and pulled out a single sheet of paper. She held it out. Jenna took it.

It was a letter from Mack, a curt, straight-to-the-point letter on plain stationery with no return address. Jenna scanned it quickly.

Dear Mrs. Kettleman,

I have decided to establish a trust fund in your name. For the next twenty years you will receive five thousand dollars per month to help cover living expenses for yourself and your family. Also, since the cost of education continues to rise, I have set up college funds for each of your four children.

Please contact the Meadow Valley office of Dennis Archer, attorney-at-law, at your earliest convenience to receive your first payment from the trust. Mr. Archer will be happy to answer any questions you may have concerning this bequest.

All my best to you and your family,

M. McGarrity

"It came today," Erin said, her voice hushed, hollow with something very close to awe. "I called that attorney. He said…" Erin closed her eyes, breathed deeply and opened them again. "He said that he'd been waiting for my call. I have an appointment for ten o'clock Monday morning. I can hardly believe it. Why? Why would he do such a thing? He doesn't even know us. We're strangers to him."

"Strangers?" Jenna smiled. *Oh, Mack,* she was thinking. *Oh, Mack. What a lovely, perfect thing to do....*

Erin Kettleman was staring at her, waiting for her to go on.

Jenna tried to explain. "I think that, in a certain way, Mack feels…very close to you and your family."

"In what way? Please tell me. Please help me to understand. It's so hard to believe that this is really happening. I keep thinking I'm gonna wake up in a few minutes and find out it's all just a crazy, impossible dream. Maybe if I knew *why* he did it…please, Ms. Bravo. You've got to tell me."

There was no resisting such a plea. Jenna didn't even try. She told Erin Kettleman of Mack's childhood, of the father he'd lost and the mother who had given him and his sisters into the care of the state. Of the funeral the two of them had attended recently in Southern California.

Erin's eyes were misty by the time the tale had been told. "How sad," she murmured. "How awful for him and his sisters—and for his mother. That poor woman. There was a time I would have judged her for what she did. But after the past six months…I think it's the worst thing that can happen to a mother, to wonder if you're going to be able to take care of your own. To find yourself thinking that maybe they'd be better off without you. Oh, that is painful. That is the worst thing in the world."

Jenna nodded. "I think he wants your family to have a better chance than his did."

"Well." Erin stood. "Thanks to him, we will."

Jenna rose and handed her the letter. Erin tucked it back into her purse. "I plan to write to him. To thank him. I suppose I can just…give the letter to the lawyer?"

Jenna understood Erin's unspoken question: *Should I give it to you?* "Yes, give it to the attorney," Jenna said firmly. "He'll know where to send it so that Mack will be sure to get it."

"Well. All right, then. I suppose I'd better get on home." Erin turned for the front door.

Jenna followed behind her, then moved past her in the foyer to open the door. The night air outside was cold. Erin shivered and wrapped her jacket closer around her.

And Jenna went ahead and asked the question she'd been wanting to ask since she'd answered the door and found Riley's mother standing on the porch. "Do you think you might bring the children by now and then? I'd love to see Riley again—and maybe hold little Lissa…."

It was Erin's turn to touch. She clasped Jenna's shoulder. "I'd love that, too." She grinned. Jenna thought she looked very young at that moment. "But I've got to warn you. They can be a handful."

"That's all right with me."

"Then I'll call you. In a week or two. We'll drop on by."

"That would be wonderful."

"Maybe Mr. McGarrity could come by, too, and—"

Jenna shook her head. "I'm afraid he's not coming back."

"Oh?" Erin let go of Jenna's shoulder. "But Riley said he thought the two of you—" Erin cut herself off, blushing a little. "Well. What does an eleven-year-old boy know, anyway?"

Jenna smiled. "He knows enough. Unfortunately, it didn't work out between me and Mr. McGarrity."

Erin sighed. "I'm sorry."

"So am I."

There was a silence. The two women regarded each other. Then Erin wrapped both arms around herself again. "You're standing here in just that light sweater. I should let you go."

"Come any time. I mean it."

Shyly, Erin promised that she would.

Jenna waited until Erin had climbed into the battered green hatchback before she closed the door. Then she leaned against the door frame, wrapped her own arms around her middle and stared down at her shoes.

She felt joy, she realized, for the Kettleman family. And pride. It was a truly fine thing that Mack had done.

She also felt sadness. Always, she felt sadness lately.

She did miss him so.

And the house seemed so quiet. She could use a little company. But the door to the back parlor was shut. It had been shut when Jenna came home from her store. Apparently Lacey was hard at work and didn't want to be disturbed.

With a sigh, Jenna pushed herself away from the wall and turned for the kitchen. She would brew herself a nice pot of tea to cut through the evening chill. And maybe in a little while Lacey would emerge from behind the louvered doors. They could share the tea and Jenna could tell her sister what Mack had done for Erin and her children.

But an hour later, Lacey's door remained firmly shut. Jenna rinsed out the teapot and went to her own room.

The next morning when Jenna entered the kitchen to fix herself some breakfast, she found the coffee brewed and her sister fully dressed, leaning on a crutch and frying eggs at the stove.

"Lace? It's seven in the morning. Are you feeling all right?"

Lacey turned her head and looked at Jenna over her shoulder. Her eyes were shining, her face flooded with excited color.

Jenna stared. "You look…terrific."

"I'm fixing breakfast," Lacey said in a strange, hushed tone. "We'll eat. And then I think it's time you saw what I've been working on." Lacey pushed a heavy lock of hair back off her face and added, "I think it's pretty good, but—" She cut herself off with a nervous shrug. "Well. Whatever you think of it, you're bound to see it sometime. Might as well get it over with."

Twenty minutes later, Jenna followed behind as her sister stumped into the back parlor.

The painting was waiting where Lacey had some-how managed to prop it, against the side of the sofa bed. Lacey gestured at it with a toss of her bright head.

"There it is," she said grimly. Then she stepped to the side and waited for Jenna's reaction.

At first, Jenna could do no more than stare.

"Well," her sister demanded after a minute. "Hit me with it. What do you think?"

Jenna didn't know what to think. It was a nude, a

male figure, and it was utterly breathtaking in its sensuality and power. A mask covered the face—a stark, simple mask that seemed carved from dark stone. In spite of the mask, Jenna knew who her sister's model had been. There was something in the tilt of the head, the shape of the shoulders—though of course, Jenna herself had never seen Lacey's subject in the nude. And she had certainly never perceived the stunning sensuality that her sister must see when she looked at him.

"You hate it," said Lacey flatly.

"No," said Jenna. "No. It is…incredible. Beautiful. Perfect."

"Oh." Lacey sucked in a breath, let it out slowly. "You think so? You honestly do?"

Jenna nodded. "Words fail me. But it's good, Lace. It's more than good."

Lacey let out another long rush of air. "You cannot know how terrific it feels to hear it from someone else—even if that someone *is* my sister who thinks everything I do is just fabulous."

"This is more than a sister's loyalty talking here, Lace. I swear to you."

"I think you mean that."

"You know I do—but I have to ask…"

Lacey closed her eyes. "I wish you wouldn't."

"Lace," Jenna said softly. "Please. Look at me."

The sisters stared at each other. Then Lacey announced, "I need to sit down."

Jenna waited as her sister hobbled to the easy chair. Once Lacey was settled, Jenna asked tentatively, "The painting… It's Logan, isn't it?"

Lacey nodded, then let out a short, slightly wild

laugh. "I warned you I might check on him, to see how he was doing, after you left."

"And I, um, take it you did."

"Did I ever. I still don't really know how it happened. I thought I was going to *comfort* him, I guess. I knew his poor heart was broken at losing you for the second time. How we ended up in bed together...well, stranger things have happened, I suppose, but not to me. It was crazy. Totally insane. It lasted for five incredible days, until I lost poor Byron and put my foot through the ceiling, which made it necessary for you and Mack to come home."

"Lace. Do you love him?"

Lacey closed her eyes again, let her head fall back against the chair. "I think I do," she said in a whisper. "Can you believe it? I think I love Logan Severance. Sometimes it seems that I might have always loved him. I just didn't realize it." Lacey opened her eyes and looked at Jenna. "He was the last person I ever thought I'd love, I swear that to you. I never had any... designs on him. Until I knocked on his door after you and Mack left town together, it never even occurred to me that maybe the animosity I'd always felt toward him was based on something else altogether. I hope you don't think that I—"

Jenna put up both hands, palm out. "Hey. It's okay. You don't have to convince me. I believe you. And you're both honorable people. Nothing would have happened between you if Logan and I had stayed together. I know that."

Byron appeared then from the door to the central hall. He strutted up to Lacey and jumped into her lap.

Lacey waited until he settled down and then scratched him behind the ears.

"Logan still loves you, Jenna."

Jenna opened her mouth to protest, but Lacey only shook her head. "It was a classic rebound situation for him, that's all."

Jenna knelt beside her sister. "No, Lacey. Listen. It's honestly over between Logan and me. And it never could have worked between us anyway."

"Tell that to Logan."

"I will. If you want me to."

"No."

"But I—"

"No. I didn't really mean that, about talking to him. Please don't say anything to him. Please just leave it alone."

"But if you love him—"

"If I love him, what?" Lacey had stiffened. Her eyes sparked with blue fire.

"Well, then you can...work things out." Jenna knew that sounded lame.

Apparently Lacey thought so, too. "Work things out?" she scoffed. "Like you and Mack did?"

Jenna had no answer for that. She stood and backed away a step. Byron, clearly uncomfortable with Lacey's sudden agitation, jumped from her lap.

"I just told you. Logan doesn't love me. He loves you—and you love Mack McGarrity, don't you?"

"Lacey, I—"

Her sister looked up at her, pure challenge in her eyes. "Don't you?"

"I..."

"For heaven's sake, will you just say it?"

"All right. Yes. I love Mack."

"And Mack loves you? Is that right?"

"Yes. He does. He loves me."

Lacey made an impatient sound. "I have to tell you, Jenna. If I thought Logan loved me, no one—and nothing—could keep me away from him. So I have to ask, what's *your* excuse?"

"Well, I… We…"

"You, we, what?"

Jenna blurted it out. "I want children. He doesn't."

Lacey frowned. "He doesn't want children…ever?"

"That's what he says."

Lacey said nothing for a count of three, then admitted grudgingly, "Well. Okay. That is a tough one."

"But I—"

"Yeah?"

"I'm willing to do without children. I do love him, Lacey. I think I'll always love him. And since last night, I've started to see that there are other ways to contribute to the raising of children than to have them yourself."

"What happened last night?"

"Remember that boy who found Byron?"

"I remember."

"Well, last night, while you were working, his mother dropped by. She told me that Mack has set up a trust fund for her, five thousand a month for the next twenty years—as well as college funds for each of her children."

Lacey gave a low whistle. "What did I say? Not the same SOB he used to be. Not the same SOB at all."

"That's right. And it's got me thinking. He's contributing to those children's lives, contributing in a very big way. And that's…important. It's, well, it could be enough for me, what we might do, together, to help other people's children grow up. And…I still love him. I'll always love him. And I miss him. And I don't want to live without him."

"Then don't. Track him down and tell him. Tell him again and again. Until he finally gives up and admits that you're the only woman in the world for him. Until he comes to his senses and confesses that he can't wait to start spending the rest of his life at your side."

Jenna stared at her sister. "You know," she said. "That's good advice."

"So take it."

Jenna dropped to the end of the sofa bed. "All right," she said. "I believe that I will."

Chapter 18

Jenna and Lacey did a lot of talking that weekend.

Lacey confessed that if Jenna wanted to sell the house their mother had left them, she would be more than glad for the extra cash. As soon as she could walk again, she intended to return to L.A. Maybe love had not worked out for her. But she was more determined than ever to fulfill her career dreams.

So they agreed. They would sell the house. They settled on a fairly low asking price, reasoning that neither of them wanted to wait forever to get on with the next phase of their lives.

Monday, Jenna visited a Realtor. She also placed an ad in the *Meadow Valley Sun,* putting her store up for sale.

Five weeks later, they got a solid offer on the house. By then it had been seven weeks since Lacey's surgery. She got a clean bill of health from her orthopedic surgeon and immediately called a friend in L.A. who invited her to stay there until she found something of her own. The next day she made arrangements to ship the painting of Logan to the artist friend with whom she'd previously shared the downtown L.A. loft.

And on Thursday, November 19, Jenna drove her sister to Sacramento International Airport.

"You don't have me to worry about anymore," Lacey said before she boarded the plane. "The house is sold and Marla can manage the store for a while. I think you'd better take a little trip to Florida. Time's passing. You need to start breaking down Mack's defenses so you can get going on the rest of your lives."

"You're absolutely right." Jenna hugged her sister.

"So? When are you leaving?"

"I'm making a plane reservation as soon as I get home."

"I'll call you the minute I get a new place—and you'd better call me and keep me posted on your love life."

"You know that I will."

"Did I tell you that you're the best sister this ex-juvenile delinquent ever had?"

"You did. So keep painting and making me proud, will you?"

"I will, I promise. I love you."

"Oh, Lace. I love you, too...."

That evening Erin Kettleman brought the kids over. They cooked hot dogs on the grill in the backyard in the rain and ate them at the breakfast nook table. Little Lissa fussed through most of the visit and Tina and the younger boy, Will, got into a spat or two. But Riley declared the meal the best he'd ever had, and all the children were thrilled to see Byron again. The cat sat in one small lap after another, purring loudly the whole time.

Before they left, Jenna told Erin that she and her cat were headed for Florida on Monday.

Erin's smile was one of pure delight. "You're getting back together with Mr. McGarrity?"

"Yes, I am," Jenna answered without a second's hesitation.

The next day, Jenna let both Marla and her other clerk have the morning off. Business was brisk, but she could handle it. In a couple of days, they'd be on their own for a while. They might as well have it a little easy until then.

At a quarter to twelve she was showing a regular customer a set of café curtains and the linens to match when she heard the bleat of the door buzzer.

She turned with her best smile ready.

And the whole world stood still.

It was Mack.

Mack.

In chinos and that sexy brown leather jacket, hands in his pockets, looking at her as if he'd like to grab her and hold her and never in a million years let her go.

"Hon?" said her customer, a thin redhead with a penchant for crinkle skirts and silver jewelry. "Hon? Are you feeling all right?"

Jenna reached out and put her hand on a nearby display rack to steady herself. "I'm just fine. Would you... excuse me?"

"Sure enough. You take your time," her customer

said, though Jenna hardly heard her. She was already walking along the towel aisle toward the man who stood a few feet from the door.

"Mack," she said when she reached him. The name had everything in it. Her love. Her longing. Her joy at the sight of him. "Hello."

He took her left hand, on which her plain wedding band gleamed, and then gently touched the cat-shaped diamond pin she wore near her heart. He smiled. Lord, how had she lived without his smile? "You're glad to see me," he said.

"*Glad* doesn't cover it. There isn't a word big enough to cover it." She drew her shoulders back. "I was coming to get you, Mack."

The light in his eyes was beautiful to see. "You were?"

"Yes. On Monday. I'm still your wife, Mack. I never took those papers in. Because I intend to remain your wife."

He said her name then, "Jenna," in a whisper, from the heart. And then he reached for her.

There were two other customers in the store besides the redhead with the silver jewelry. One of them gasped, the other said, "Ahh…" And the redhead murmured, "How sweet."

Neither Mack nor Jenna cared what her customers thought. They kissed for a long time, a kiss of true reunion, a kiss between man and wife.

At last he lifted his head, but he still held her close, right against his heart.

He said, "I did it, Jenna. I went to see both of my sisters."

"Oh, Mack…"

"And they are two very nice women. Bridget has three happy, loud, normal kids. And Claire is pregnant with her first baby. It's going to be a girl. I… Well, I think if they can do it, maybe I can do it, too."

"Mack. Are you saying…?"

He nodded. "I'm terrified, scared out of my wits. But yes. I'll do it. I'll have a family with you. It feels like the biggest damn chance I'll ever take in my life. But I'm good at taking risks…right?"

"You are, Mack. You take chances. And those chances pay off."

"You really didn't file the papers?"

"No."

"And you really want to stay my wife?"

"Yes."

"I don't even have to beg you or get down on my knees?"

"Well, a little begging *would* be nice…."

He yanked her close again and called her a naughty name. Then he kissed her for the second time.

And he said, "I love you."

And she said, "I love you, too. So much. So very much…"

And right then the buzzer rang again. It was Marla, ready for work.

"Do you think you could handle things here on your own for a while?" Jenna asked.

Marla said that she could. So Jenna grabbed her purse and her coat and she and Mack left the store. They walked hand in hand to the Queen Anne Victorian at the top of West Broad Street.

Byron was waiting just inside the front door. Mack scooped Jenna up and carried her straight to the master bedroom on the first floor. The cat followed behind them, purring quite loudly, his long black tail held high and proud.

A few weeks later, Mack and Jenna renewed their vows in Florida aboard Mack's boat, *The Shady Deal.* Mack flew the guests in. Lacey was there, and Mack's sisters and their families, and Alec and Lois, and the entire Kettleman clan.

After the ceremony Jenna and Mack left for a second honeymoon. They went to Wyoming. Jenna met the children of her grandfather's brother. And in the years to come, she always insisted that they conceived their first child there, on the ranch that had been in the Bravo family for five generations.

* * * * *

FAMOUS FAMILIES

YES! Please send me the *Famous Families* collection featuring the Fortunes, the Bravos, the McCabes and the Cavanaughs. This collection will begin with 3 FREE BOOKS and 2 FREE GIFTS in my very first shipment—and more valuable free gifts will follow! My books will arrive in 8 monthly shipments until I have the entire 51-book *Famous Families* collection. I will receive 2-3 free books in each shipment and I will pay just $4.49 U.S./$5.39 CDN for each of the other 4 books in each shipment, plus $2.99 for shipping and handling.* If I decide to keep the entire collection, I'll only have paid for 32 books because 19 books are free. I understand that accepting the 3 free books and gifts places me under no obligation to buy anything. I can always return a shipment and cancel at any time. My free books and gifts are mine to keep no matter what I decide.

268 HCN 9971   468 HCN 9971

Name _____ (PLEASE PRINT)

Address _____ Apt. #

City _____ State/Prov. _____ Zip/Postal Code

Signature (if under 18, a parent or guardian must sign)

Mail to the **Reader Service:**

IN U.S.A.: P.O. Box 1867, Buffalo, NY 14240-1867
IN CANADA: P.O. Box 609, Fort Erie, Ontario L2A 5X3

FFBPA11